Groan.

The sound was deep and throaty, almost like the sound of a man...well, getting off.

She cupped her hands over her mouth. *I can't believe this guy.* The clock was ticking and it was really rude to keep someone waiting so he could wank it.

She gave the door another hard knock. "Listen, buddy, if you're doing anything but dying, you'd better open this door, or I'm leaving. And I'm pretty sure you don't want that."

The man groaned again, but this time the sound was so deep and hard, it sent shivers up her spine and down to her nether region. His voice was just so damned sexy.

What? Sadie, what's wrong with you?

"Oh. Come on, buddy!" Knock. Knock. Knock. "Can't you do that later?"

She suddenly heard some rustling and then the sound of something large thumping on the floor. The door flew open and a huge man, wearing partially unzipped leather pants, stood panting in the doorway, no underwear, his pants barely holding to his hips and slung low on his muscular torso. She could see a dark patch of hair and the base of his cock, which looked hard as hell, straining against the inside of his pants.

She gulped. The man was hung.

Her eyes moved up over the snug fabric of his black T-shirt, the muscles of his chest and arms stretching it to its limits. She was sure this guy was some sort of weight lifter or martial arts enthusiast. *Or the next Thor.* Just like Bob had said.

When her eyes finally got to his face, two intense turquoise eyes burned right through her, stopping her breath for several heartbeats until her brain registered the fact that it was the same face who'd visited her the last two evenings in two unwelcome, very erotic dreams.

"So we meet again, meat wench." His sinful lips flashed a smug little smile. "Why am I not surprised to see you here begging for more?"

OTHER WORKS BY MIMI JEAN PAMFILOFF:

FATE BOOK (New Adult Suspense/Humor)
FATE BOOK TWO (New Adult Suspense/Humor)
THE HAPPY PANTS CAFÉ (Prequel/Romantic Comedy)

THE KING TRILOGY (Dark Fantasy)
King's (Book 1)
King for a Day (Book 2)
King of Me (Book 3)

THE MERMEN TRILOGY (Dark Fantasy)
Mermen (Book 1)
MerMadmen (Book 2)

IMMORTAL

MATCHMAKERS, INC.

Mimi Jean Pamfiloff

a Mimi Boutique Novel

To: Jessica

Hope you liked the book I picked for you!

Ebook ISBN: 978-0-9962504-1-2
PRINT ISBN: 978-0-9962504-2-9

Cover Design by EarthlyCharms.com
Editing by Latoya C. Smith and Pauline Nolet
Formatting by WriteIntoPrint.com

Like "FREE" Pirated Books?
Then Ask Yourself This Question:
WHO ARE THESE PEOPLE I'M HELPING?

What sort of person or organization would put up a website that uses stolen work (or encourages its users to share stolen work) in order to make money for themselves, either through website traffic or direct sales?

Haven't you ever wondered?

Putting up thousands of pirated books onto a website or creating those anonymous ebook file sharing sites takes time and resources. Quite a lot, actually.

So who are these people? Do you think they're decent, ethical people with good intentions? Why do they set up camp anonymously in countries where they can't easily be touched? And the money they make from advertising every time you go to their website, or through selling stolen work, **what are they using it for?**

The answer is you don't know.

They could be terrorists, organized criminals, or just greedy bastards. But one thing we DO know is that **THEY ARE CRIMINALS** who don't care about you, your family, or me and mine.

And their intentions can't be good.

And every time you illegally share or download a book, YOU ARE HELPING these people. Meanwhile, people like me, who work to support a family and children, are left wondering why anyone would condone this.

So please, please ask yourself who YOU are HELPING when you support ebook piracy and then ask yourself who you are HURTING.

And for those who legally purchased or borrowed or obtained my work from a reputable retailer (not sure, just ask me!) muchas thank yous! You rock.

DEDICATION

To Bridget and Ally. Thank you for your insane passion for this series (especially Cimil), for your love of unicorn paraphernalia, for the fun you bring to the street team, for the exuberance you show for life, and for being awesome human beings. You make the world a better place.

WARNING:

This book contains F-bombs, unicorns, leather pants, vampires, insane deities, hot assassins, and many references to extremely large penises. If you do not like F-bombs, unicorns, leather pants, vampires, insane deities, hot assassins, or large penises then this story is likely not for you.

IMMORTAL
MATCHMAKERS, INC.

My Dearest People Pets:

I'm back, bitches! Did ya miss me? Did ya, did ya, huh? Don't answer that! Of course you did! And you've been counting the seconds, longing restlessly for my horribly inappropriate insanity. Well, wait no further! Auntie Cimi knows exactly what you want: A quiz! So without further ado, I giveth the quizeth:

1. Dear gods, I am so very grateful that Mimi has decided to write a spin-off of the Accidentally Yours Series because:

A. It gives me an excuse to continue sending Mimi unicorn-themed items (such as hand-crocheted hats, earrings, headbands with uni-horns, stickers, socks, "I don't believe in humans" T-shirts, "I fucking love unicorns" pint glasses, and underwear) as well as all of the unicorn-related posts I find on Facebook.

B. It did not sit well with me that Andrus, Tommaso, Belch (the God of Wine), Bees, the Goddess of Forgetfulness, Gabran, K'ak, Zac, Sentin, and all of the other immortals I've grown to love have not found their mates. Where's the justice in that?!

C. I do not buy for one moment that Cimil can be reformed, but I'm excited to watch her try.

D. Men in leather pants with turquoise eyes make me wetter than a tadpole.

2. I predict that during the IMMORTAL MATCHMAKERS, INC., series, we will discover the following about Minky the unicorn:

    A. She's not real and never has been.

    B. She dreams of becoming a porn star.

    C. She is secretly in love with one of the gods.

    D. Minky isn't a unicorn, but another species enslaved by Cimil for her own personal amusement.

3. Cimil hates clowns because:

    A. They are evil.

    B. They are evil.

    C. They are evil.

Okay, y'all. The quizeth has concludedeth. You may find the answers in the back of the book! And I do hope you enjoy my journey of restitution for all that I have done wrong. (Hahaha! You wish I cared! Okay, I secretly do. Don't tell.)

Accidentally Mine,

Cimil, Goddess of the Underworld

PS—Minky sends her invisible regards.

CHAPTER ONE

"Godsdammit. I'm going to need a snack." Zac, God of Temptation and the most awesome motherfucking badass deity on the planet, took his Bionic Man lunchbox from his black leather backpack, placed it on his desk, and went for his bologna sandwich.

"Fuck. Me. This can't be happening," he whispered and tore off a big bite while staring at the computer screen. *One hundred and fifty?* They hadn't even been open for a day.

His computer made that strange little swoosh sound, indicating more of this "email" crap was flowing into his "inbox."

He took another bite and nearly choked. "What the bloody hell?" Now two hundred and eighty immortals had filled out the online request form.

He looked over his shoulder, across the empty space of the twentieth floor, which they'd rented in downtown L.A. The big corner office remained empty.

Traitor.

It was well past noon, yet his crazy fucking redheaded mess of a sister Cimil, The Goddess of the Underworld, was nowhere to be found on their official first day of business. Of course, she'd insisted on getting the only office because she was "critical to mankind's survival."

What a bunch of deity-crap. As far as he was concerned, they were both equally valuable to humanity and both in this mess for two reasons: One, she was bat-shit crazy. And two, he'd trusted her. Having to open this matchmaking agency for immortals was all her goddamned fault.

That's right. My only crime was falling in love with my brother's woman. Yeah, so maybe he'd crossed a few lines, using his powers to try (and fail) to break them up. But banishment by the other gods to this hellhole of traffic, smog, and heat they called "Los Angeles"? Then having to come to this enormous, soul-sucking coffin of glass and steel—called an "office building"—every day to work like some lowly mortal slave to assist the unlaid immortal masses?

No fucking gracias, amigos.

His eyes darted around the empty space, taking note of its tragically undignified decorum of white walls, gray carpet, and artificial lighting. *Maybe I can spruce up the place with some paintings of naked women and chocolate—tempting shit like that.*

He shoved the rest of his sandwich into his mouth, dusted off his hands on his black leather pants, and went back to his computer, toggling through the profiles. *Vampire, vampire, demigod, my brother, my other brother, Uchben, immortal warrior...unicorn?*

"Hi. Are you Zac?" said a sweet, feminine voice.

He looked up and found a short woman with a long blonde ponytail and big blue eyes, standing in the doorway, looking very nervous. Her petite body, though covered in a horribly unrevealing dress with disgusting flowers all over it, was cute and curvy.

She batted her big blues in question.

He held up his index finger and swallowed down the lump of food. "Yeah, I'm Zac. Who the hell are you?" She appeared human, but this was a matchmaking agency for immortals only.

With an eager, friendly smile she approached, holding out her hand. "I'm Tula Jones. So nice to meet you."

He stood from his chair and watched her gaze follow his face up, up, up.

Her mouth fell open. "She wasn't lying; you really are big."

Of course. He was a deity—one of fourteen, over seventy thousand years old, and seven feet of masculine perfection right down to his godsdamned dingle berries. Not that he had any, because he was far too perfect for that shit.

Zac crossed his powerful arms over his magnificent chest. "Yes, I am big. In many, many ways." He cocked a suggestive brow, wondering how many seconds it would take her to reach out and touch him. The ladies always wanted a little feel. "So which lucky lady sent you?" It wasn't uncommon for the women to talk after an exquisite night with him. A god. A badass god. With a huge cock. And he'd been plowing a whole hell of a lot of mortal fields these past few weeks. Hell, what else was there to do? Cry over his broken, banished, badass heart? No fucking way.

"Uh, well," she said meekly, "your sister Cimil told me about you. Said I shouldn't be afraid or let you push me around."

Cimil sent me a woman to fuck? This Tula was a bit small for his taste, around five feet or so, but she looked like she might know her way around a cock. Maybe this day was looking up.

"She hired me to be your assistant," Tula added, her nervous eyes continuing to scale up and down his body.

Oh. So no afternoon booty delivery, huh? Maybe he'd go next door to the Starbucks and pick someone up. Banished and powerless or not, he was still a deity and completely irresistible to women. What his body didn't catch, his scent did. One whiff and the ladies swarmed like horny bees.

"And what makes my sister think I need an assistant?" he said skeptically.

"Your sister said, and I quote, 'He is a giant asshat and completely useless, so he needs someone to do everything for him.'"

He wasn't an asshat. An asshole, maybe. But

either way, was Cimil out of her immortal skull? Humans were on a need-to-know basis because they usually freaked the fuck out about the immortal community. They'd have everything from vampires to that nightmare of a head case, Cimil's unicorn, coming through on a daily basis.

Tula added, "She also mentioned that you might need some cheering up and moral support. And, wow, she was right about your hair."

"My hair?" He ran his hand over the length of his shaggy black mane.

"She said it screamed depression. Want me to book you a salon appointment?" Tula asked.

What? His hair did not scream "depression." It looked shiny and unkempt and screamed "badass!" The women constantly complimented him on how it set off his turquoise eyes.

Of course, they're usually looking at the bulge in my pants when they say it.

"I'm sorry," he said, growling, "but I think there's been a mistake. We're not hiring."

"Uh-huh," Tula said cheerily. "Should I sit here?" She walked around the desk and slid her petite frame past his body, sending a hard spike of arousal through his groin. She took the seat he'd just been in and looked up at him, smiling sassily.

"What are you doing?" he said.

"Your sister also explained that you'd try to run me off. Because, and I quote, 'He's a giant asshat and thinks he's too awesome to need help from anyone.'"

He growled and reached for her. "Okay, little girl, it's time for you—"

She leaned away from his hand. "Please don't kick me out. I really need this job."

He froze and then dropped his hand. *Godsdammit.* "My sister told you to say that, didn't she?"

Tula shook her head. "No. But it's the truth. I need the money for college. I've only got one more year left, and my parents can't afford the tuition. This is the only job I've been able to find that comes close to paying the bills and is flexible enough for me to go to school."

Bloody fucking hell. She'd found his loophole. No, he didn't mean his asshole—his loophole. A deity's purpose was to help humans. It was hardwired into their DNA from day one.

Now he had to help.

He scratched his unshaven jaw, unsure of what to do with her. Why would Cimil hire this naïve little human female to help them pay their penance—finding mates for one hundred immortals—or something like that? Honestly, the other garble the other gods had said at his sentencing about learning compassion and the true meaning of love had gone in one ear and out the other. The part about being stripped of his powers and banished, however? Well, that stuck like dog shit on a shoe.

"Fine," he grumbled. "You can stay. But just for the time being until you find another job."

"Thank you! Thank you," she said. "I promise you won't be disappointed. I'm a hard worker and great at organizing."

"Yes. Yes. You're welcome. You're welcome," he said blandly. Now where would he sit? He looked around the empty room that would also serve as their lobby. "I'll work in there." *Fuck Cimil.* She hadn't shown, so he'd take the big office. Let her sit on the floor. "Maybe you can start by ordering some…" He waved his hand in the air. "Some things to make this hellhole look less like a hellhole." Gods only knew how long he'd have to keep coming here; might as well make it worthy of a deity.

"Okay. I'll get right on it." She glanced down at the desk. "Is that a Bionic Man lunch pail?"

"Yes." *Silly mortal.* Could she not see the giant letters on the metal box, clearly stating "The Bionic Man"?

"My dad had one of those when he was little. A huge Bionic Man fan," she said.

Her father? But the woman at the very "cool and hip" store for younger humans had said that it was what the "edgy" and "fucking awesome" people used these days to transport their afternoon meals. No, he didn't have to eat but enjoyed doing it anyway. Yes, he was a stress eater.

Okay? Even deities had their challenges. *Thankfully, I don't gain weight. I'm just a giant piece of awesome.*

Zac looked down at the lunch box and rubbed his jaw. "Well, it's a...a friend gave it to me as a joke." *Note to badass self: Must smite salesperson at trendy store for deceiving me.*

"Aww...well, I think it's cute," she said.

In that case, I will merely maim salesperson.

Tula scooted her body closer to the desk. "So, where would you like me to start after I order the furniture?" She flashed a smile that, despite its nervousness, was bright and cheery. Of course, that happy shit was completely lost on him.

"Ehhh...well, what exactly did my sister tell you?"

"Um, that you are the God of Temptation—now exiled and powerless—and she is the Goddess of the Underworld, also exiled, though she still communes with the dead. She is also a new mother to two boys and two girls, and, I quote, 'one dangerous mess of woman-hormones with giant cow udders.'"

"She told you what we are?" he asked. "And you're not afraid?"

She shook her head, her blonde ponytail flopping side to side. "No, sir. My momma raised me with an open mind, and I always suspected there was more to this world than what I saw with my eyes." She shrugged. "I love being right."

Funny. Me too!

"Ah, well. In that case, Tula, welcome to reality."

She leaned forward, lacing her hands together. "So is it true? You have an army of immortal warriors, kind of like the bad vampires in the *Twilight* book?"

He cringed. "We are gods. Fourteen of the most powerful creatures in existence, not…" He made a sour face. "Vampires." Of course, in general he didn't have anything against those sneaky sifting bastards. For example, his brother Kinich, ex-God of the Sun, was now a vampire, and even Cimil's mate, Roberto, was an Ancient One—the first of his kind. He was also once an Egyptian pharaoh, which made him an arrogant, ruthless fucker. Who could resist liking that?

He added, "We are divine, my dear human. Birthed from the Universe's womb."

She shrugged. "I still loved *Twilight*."

He gave her a look and was about to speak when he noticed something unexpected: Her aura.

Holy fuck. What. Is. That? In his seventy thousand years, he'd never seen a human with a purer soul. Not one. Looking at her was like gazing at a patch of newly fallen snow.

"You okay, Mr. Zac?" she asked.

He nodded dumbly.

"'Cause you look like you want to put whatever you just ate right back in the Bionic Man box." She scooted the lunch pail closer to him.

He shook his head. *So pure. So...wholesome. So...going to fucking kill Cimil!*

"Could you excuse me one moment?" He held up his finger, and she gave him a nod.

He marched into the empty office, dug out his cellphone, and dialed Cimil. As it rang, he closed the door.

"Hayyyyy looooow. This is Cimil. You've reached my voicemail because I'm busy licking Roberto's enormous sarcophagus or I'm allowing these tiny helpless degenerates to suckle from my ample teets or I'm plotting the destruction of mankind. Please leave a message and I will call you back as soon as never." *Beep.*

Zac growled into his phone before letting loose. "Cimil, I'm going to dismember you. First, you betray me. Then I'm banished. Now...*now* you hire a human who's, who's..." He couldn't say the words.

"Who's what?" said a voice from behind him.

Zac swiveled in his black leather biker boots to find Cimil. She wore a pair of pink lederhosen, gold platform shoes and her flaming red hair in an enormous bun on the top of her head. Her T-shirt read "God Milk?" and had two arrows, one pointing to each breast. Honestly, he still found it disturbing to think of Cimil as a mother. Worst of all, those babies had such an evil vibe. When he'd met them, he could've sworn he'd heard Satanic chanting coming from their cribs.

"Where the hell have you been?" he growled. "And what the hell do you think you're up to?"

Her turquoise eyes—the exact same color as his and the other deities—shifted around the room. "I am getting ready to serve my time for my crimes. Boy, we really need to get some color going in here. What do you think of a clown theme?"

He noticed Tula peeking behind Cimil.

"I'm talking about the human," he whispered.

"She is our employee," Cimil whispered back.

"Don't fuck with me. You're up to something."

"Why would I be up to something?"

"Because you're Cimil."

"Good point. But I assure you that Tula is our helper and nothing more. She's also taken, Zac, head over heels in love with a nice young human man named Gilbert whom she is to marry."

Oh great. Even worse. After all, he was the God of Temptation, and stripped powers or not, he was who he was. He liked tempting people. He liked it a whole hell of a lot. And Cimil had hired a human who'd be irresistible to him. He'd want to tempt her every which way possible.

"And," Cimil added, "because her heart is so pure, she's in no danger from you."

Zac lifted a brow, still not believing Cimil.

"Okay. So." Cimil clapped her hands together. "That was a tough workday. See you tomorrow!"

"You've been here all of two minutes, Cimil. And I don't know about you, but I want my punishment over as fast as possible." Living in the mortal world without any powers was already beginning to grind on him. How did his brethren who voluntarily spent their time in this world stand it? It felt like being confined in a small box. *I much prefer the freedom of our realm and being disembodied.*

Cimil tilted her head, studying him with curiosity.

"Why are you looking at me like that?" he asked.

She stared for another long moment and then her eyes widened in shock.

"Cimil?" He snapped his fingers, but she remained zoned out. *Oh great.* He hated when she did that because it usually indicated she was having a vision or an incoming message from the dead. Generally neither were good. "What, dammit?"

She blinked. "Woo! That was horrifying." She shook her head from side to side. "Zac, are you feeling a little agitated lately?"

"Your abilities to discern the obvious are impressive. What did you just see?"

"I'm not certain, but I sensed something is going to be wrong with you."

"Yes. And its name is Cimil. That's definitely it." And knowing he'd be stuck in the human world for a very, very long time while having to be around that little temptress Tula. How would he get anything done around here? He'd be obsessing over how to corrupt her. And help her, too, of course. Because he was a god and needed to help humans. Yes, they were all quite fucked up.

Cimil puckered her bright red lips, looking genuinely concerned—a rarity. "I have a feeling that this sentence of ours is not going to be easy on you, dear Zac. So given the kind and generous sister I am, I'll hurry things along. Which makes it very convenient that I've identified the first client and laid out the entire game plan to avoid any hurdles, including recruiting—or blackmailing—same diff—our client's BFF. *Victimo numero uno* is as good as in the bag."

Okay. This was good. *Only ninety-nine more immortals to match up.*

She continued, "So I suggest to make things move faster, I focus on our first client while you work with Tula there to set up a mixer. We can throw a wild lovefest for all of the eligible immortals looking for love."

"Oh." Zac rubbed his chin. An immortal singles mixer would surely result in a shitload of matches. *It's fucking genius.* Not that he would admit that to Cimil. *But she does have her moments.*

"Now, get out," she said. "I don't want anyone in my office. Lots of confidential stuff lying around."

There was nothing but a cold computer and an empty desk.

"You're not getting this office," he said.

"Hey, it's the least you can offer after everything I've done for you," she squabbled.

"You mean the fact that I'm being punished because you lied and manipulated me?" She'd promised everything would work out with his brother's woman if he followed her advice. Of course, Cimil claimed everything *had* worked out. Just not for him.

"Exactly." She shrugged happily. "And stop your whining. I got banished, too, and the only thing I did was tell a few lies, torture a few innocent souls, and save the world from ending. How fair is that?"

"Uh, because you were secretly driving the world to its end at the same time?" Of course, she couldn't really help it. Like him, she had her dark side, but ultimately served the greater good. Very twisted.

That Universe and her sense of humor. What a riot.

"Now shoo!" She swept her hands through the air. "Minky needs her rest."

Zac shook his head. Minky was Cimil's pet, a bloodthirsty and invisible unicorn. It was better not to speak of such things.

He followed Cimil out, and she closed the door behind her and locked it. "Okay. I have my womba class—boy, those four little monsters really stretched the old uterus right out—then Roberto and I have our daddy-vampire and mommy-goddess class. See you both tomorrow."

Zac was about to ask about the class, but then realized he didn't give a fuck.

"Tootles!" Cimil said, wiggling her pale gaunt fingers in the air. "And keep your paws off Tula! She's taken!"

Dammit, Cimil. She knew that saying that would make him want her more. He hoped she was joking about the taken part.

"Wait," he said. "You never told me who our first 'in the bag' client is."

She flashed a devilish grin over her shoulder. "The infamous Andrus Gray."

Oh, hell. That guy? Definitely not in the bag. "If that's the case, then we are going to need his best friend's help."

CHAPTER TWO

New York City

Andrus Gray gazed down into Helena's sky-blue eyes, the hate and rage bubbling off her face like overheating spaghetti sauce.

This was bad. Very bad. But not his fault. Did she not understand that?

"I can't believe you, Andrus. And in my own home, too? Get. Out," she growled, pointing toward the steel-reinforced door of the lavish penthouse.

She was going to blame him? *Him?* Of course, what should he expect? She wasn't going to fault the real culprit for starting the fight: her husband, Niccolo DiConti.

Andrus knew she loved them both, but Niccolo was her mate and he was merely the "manny," aka bodyguard slash nanny. Still, he had fucking hoped she would choose him regardless of the improbability. *At the very least, I expected her to side with me.*

She hadn't.

Niccolo entered the room with a familiar black duffle bag. "Here's your shit. Now get out," he said with a scowl he'd perfected over thirteen hundred years. "She—correction—*we* don't want you here anymore."

Andrus glanced out at the spitefully sunny, panoramic view of Central Park, biting down on his tongue and trying not to lose his cool. Truth was, he'd fucked up because he'd known this arrangement was a mistake from day one. Niccolo—once a vampire but now a demigod like himself—had been away, working with the gods to stop some ridiculous end-of-world rubbish. Meanwhile, Cimil—crazy, untrustworthy goddess—had had a vision foretelling of an attack on Helena and her soon-to-come baby while Niccolo was away. As luck so had it, Andrus had been the only immortal warrior qualified to protect Helena in his absence.

And...you owed her a considerable apology. A long story, and partially why he had agreed to take the role, but Andrus had once kidnapped Helena, wishing to use her as a pawn when they first met. Then she grew on him while being his captive. Everything worked out for the best in the end more or less—*less*—however, he hadn't been able to say no to assisting Helena after all that he'd done to the woman. Even if it meant taking on the demeaning task of watching over her infant once it arrived.

But then she came.

Little Matty.

The sweetest, smartest child in the world, with

golden locks the color of sunshine, hopeful blue eyes that reminded him of his long departed sister, and laughter made from pure joy—the kind he once knew before he was made immortal against his will. He laid eyes on Matty and immediately loved her like his own. He didn't even mind that the other immortal men made fun of him for being the manny. Nor did he mind when the child bit him, which happened quite frequently because she had Helena's vampire blood. Little Matty had given him a peace he hadn't known for over three hundred years.

And now, it's over. For something that wasn't his fault. *Niccolo crossed the line. I merely reacted.* Of course, that didn't matter to Helena. She had a very strict no violence rule inside their home.

"May I say goodbye to Matty?" he asked, looking only at Helena. If he looked at Niccolo, he would end up throwing a punch. Again. Because the man was a smug son of a bitch who thought he could treat him like a servant.

I am a fucking assassin, goddammit. Over three hundred years old, infused with the divine light of the gods, trained to hunt and kill evil vampires.

Helena growled under her breath and then jerked her head toward Matty's room. "Make it quick."

Andrus walked to the nursery, where Matty still napped in her favorite dress—the one with a fangy pink bat on the front. He didn't want to wake her, but he needed to hold her one last time.

He gently scooped the little girl, almost two years old now, into his arms and cradled her to his chest. He buried his nose in her blonde curls, inhaling her sweet scent. "I love you, little one. Don't ever forget that. Uncle Andrus will always be here for you if you ever need anything."

He felt his dark immortal heart tearing in two. But if he stayed, he and Niccolo would end up killing each other. And as much as he despised the man, Niccolo was Matty's biological father. He did not want to be responsible for detaching the bastard's fat head.

Andrus laid Matty back down, took one last look at her, and sighed. When he turned, he saw Helena standing in the doorway, her eyes filled with tears. Niccolo stood behind her, still snarling like the considerable prick that he was.

Bastard. He doesn't deserve Helena. Couldn't he see that his jealousy was hurting her? And fucking prick that he was, he refused to give even a modicum of appreciation. It didn't have to end like this. Niccolo made it so.

"Would it kill you to simply show a little gratitude, Niccolo? For once in your long, pathetic existence?" *Thank you for looking after Helena and Matty? Thank you for acting like a gentleman and never once making a pass at Helena?* Or at least, since those two got married. He lived by a code of honor.

"Thank you, Andrus," Helena said. "Thank you for making sure Matty and I were safe while Niccolo," she elbowed Niccolo in the ribs, "was away."

Well, at least Helena has some class. But that wasn't so unusual. It was one of the reasons he adored her.

Niccolo grunted. "Hey, I was fighting to save the world from destruction. You should be thanking *me*."

Helena rolled her eyes and looked at Andrus. "We're *both* grateful."

Andrus bobbed his head. "Goodbye. And...my best wishes for the baby on the way." It was the final slap in the face: Helena was four months pregnant with Matty's little sister. He would not get to be there to see her first few hours of life or watch the look on Matty's sweet tiny face when she first held her baby sister.

Because you're nothing to them. You never have been.

He slid past Helena and Niccolo, using every ounce of restraint he could muster to not go at it with Niccolo again.

He walked out the front door with his supply of leather pants, his weapons, and a few personal grooming items; however, the only thing worth taking was a picture of him and Matty playing samurai—yes, with real swords—never too young to learn the fine art of decapitation—which he always carried with him.

He rode the elevator from the penthouse down to the lobby, managing to maintain his calm, disciplined air; meanwhile his insides were a fucking mess.

When he walked outside, it was an unusually warm late October day, and it occurred to him he had nowhere to go. He had money, more than enough to last an eternity, but he had no real home unless he counted his family's old castle outside of St. Petersburg, Russia.

No. Filled with too many sad memories. His family had long since perished. Every last one of them. *Fuck it. I'll go get my Hummer out of storage and drive to Miami.*

His phone rang the second he held up his hand for a taxi.

He slid the device from his pocket and saw the caller ID displayed "Tommaso," another demigod— not born that way, but infused with the light of the gods—like him. Really, all that meant was they were immortal and tougher to kill. No real superpowers.

"What is up?" Andrus grumbled curtly.

"Hey, bro," Tommaso said with a slight Italian accent. "I need a favor. And do not fucking tell me you can't get time off from watching Matty. Niccolo is back."

Yes, no shit. "What do you want?"

"Come out to L.A."

"For?" Andrus asked. He'd already set his mind on someplace warm and tropical where he might do some spearfishing, kill something pretty, and pretend it was Niccolo.

"Just get on a fucking plane and get out here. I need you for a few days."

First off, he loathed flying. It felt unnatural to be tens of thousands of feet up in the air. "I am not putting my ass inside one of those mortal death traps simply so you can tell me what you want." With his luck, it would be some inane errand for Cimil. "Wait. Isn't Cimil in Los Angeles?"

"Yeah. So?"

Tommaso was the sort of man who excelled at the art of manipulation—not a warrior like himself. More like a pretty boy who favored fine suits and stylish hair. Nevertheless, they had grown to be friends over the past year or so, for one simple reason: they'd both been branded traitors. Of course, they also had their reasons for the things they'd done, which was why they were allowed to live and pay their dues. But they would forever be branded as bad boys of the immortal community. Given the community was made up of some fairly vicious vampires, the gods' human army (known as Uchben), a variety of dangerous and predatory immortals, and fourteen of the most insane, dysfunctional, fucked-up deities that made circus folk look like preppies, it said a lot that he and

Tommaso had been deemed the "messed up" ones.

"So why are you there?" Andrus asked.

"I, uh…"

"You're having Cimil and Zac set you up, aren't you?" Andrus asked.

"No. They're setting *you* up. Zac and Cimil just called and asked if I could get you on board since we all know you're a little…"

"A little what?" he snarled.

"Stubborn, uncivilized, ruthless, and cold. Then there's the fact you like killing things and carry around a blood-crusted sword and you look like you might tear off anyone's head if they so much as look at you the wrong way and—"

"I always clean my sword after I kill something, and I'm not going on a fucking date." A) other than a one-night fuck here and there, he didn't want anything to do with women. And, B) he didn't want anything to do with Cimil.

"Drus, come on. It's one date. That's all."

"How the hell did Zac and Cimil get you in on this? What do you get out of it?" Andrus asked.

Silence.

"Fine. I'm hanging up now," Andrus grumbled.

"Cimil said she knows who my mate is. She'll introduce us at some big party they're throwing if I get you out to L.A. and convince you to go on a date."

Andrus growled. He didn't have time for this

shit. Okay. He did. But he wasn't in the mood for one of Cimil's goddamned shenanigans that always led to something bad. After all, she was insane.

"Regrettably, Tommaso," Andrus replied, "I cannot right now. I have some things to figure out." Like how to get over losing Matty and Helena from his life.

"I know Helena kicked you out," Tommaso said.

"How the hell do you know that?" *It happened…what? Two minutes ago?*

"How do you think?"

Cimil. She and her goddamned dead. Everyone used to think she saw the future, but really, she just spoke to the dead who lived in some other plane where time didn't exist. People who had not been born were already there because some time in the future, they would die. It was extremely fucking confusing.

"Tell Cimil and her garrulous deceased to stay out of my life," Andrus growled.

"Sorry, man; we're talking Cimil here. That's impossible. But she says the woman is really hot."

"What's the point? I had a mate once. She died. Do you not recall?" *Then I met Helena, and she'll never be mine.*

"That's why you need to come to L.A.," Tommaso said. "She said the Universe has granted you another chance."

The Universe didn't do that. It was one mate per immortal. Cimil was probably up to something.

Something no one could anticipate because she was too insane to follow any logical motives.

"Sounds like a hoax," Andrus grumbled.

"There's only one way to find out: meet the woman. You'll know the second you set eyes on her."

Andrus's heart started to pound in his chest. He'd not been lucky in the love department, and he specifically referred to his now deceased mate, Reyna, the evil vampire queen who'd hijacked his life over three hundred years ago. The deceitful, mad shrew had allowed the evil vampire population to explode, which angered the gods. When they threatened to kill her, she traded his life along with some of her best warriors in exchange for her own. But before she handed them over to be infused with the light of the gods, she made him like the rest of her men—a vampire. They would then become known as the Demilords—a new species of warrior that was stronger, faster, unaffected by the sun, and did not require blood for sustenance. The ultimate killing machines. But as long as evil vampires roamed the earth, they would be under the command of the gods.

The men would eventually declare him their leader when he vowed to free them all, but it took three long centuries before they'd see the end to their servitude and have their vampire ties severed with the death of Reyna.

A giant cluster fuck, to be sure. The moral of the story, however, was that freedom was a good thing, and love—the true kind—had evaded him his entire life.

"What have you got to lose, Andrus?" Tommaso urged.

My freedom. My sanity. "Everything."

A moment of silence passed. "Andrus, Helena will never love you. Not the way you want and need her to. And I know you still have hang-ups about Reyna."

No. Really? "What is your point, Tommaso?"

"That you're talented at many things—mostly killing—but moving on isn't one of your strengths. And if you don't change that, you'll stay stuck exactly where you are."

"The way I see it, that's my problem. No one else's."

"Really? Because the way I see it, you've made it Helena and Matty's too. You should've left months ago once Niccolo got back."

"They asked me to stay," Andrus argued.

"To be polite, man. Helena didn't want to run you off like that; she cares about you. But you and I both know you should've left—two alphas can't share the same house, especially when they're both in love with the same woman and one of them is not the husband."

Tommaso's cruel words felt like an arrow right through the heart. Mostly because they were all true, right down to the fact that he and Niccolo had just gone at it. Of course, it was all a misunderstanding on Niccolo's arrogant part, but still.

Tommaso went on, "Come to L.A., Andrus. Do it before you find yourself hovering outside her building, fighting the urge to be near them and protect them."

Andrus blinked, turned, and looked straight up at the tall building. *Sonofabitch. I'm standing guard outside.* Tommaso was right. He couldn't keep hanging on to his hope that Helena would want him. It was time to start trying to let go of his past. The only issue was, without those two things, he didn't quite know who he was anymore.

You're a lethal assassin. A demigod. What else is there to know?

"Fine," Andrus replied. "See you tomorrow. Text me the address."

CHAPTER THREE

As the last slice of sun sank into the waves, Andrus pulled up in his black Hummer—an airport rental, but still his usual ride—to the small seafood restaurant overlooking the Pacific Ocean. He flipped down the vanity mirror and ran his hands through his short spiky dark hair, questioning if he should have shaved. Or showered. Or bothered to change his clothes.

Nah. If this woman was truly his mate, she would be instantly turned on. And not like he smelled bad. Not really. Although, he did wear his lucky leather pants, but those smelled of victory. He had killed at least seven hundred evil vampires while wearing them.

All right. I probably should've worn the pants without the bloodstains. At least he'd brushed his teeth at the airport. All right, he'd gargled with whisky. So what? Matty loved his whisky breath. Of course, she was a toddler and enjoyed drinking blood, so her definition of good breath probably wasn't the same as most.

He exited the vehicle, swiping his leather duster from the backseat and then slipped a blade sheathed in leather down the back of his pants. One could never be too prepared for danger.

He strolled into the upscale restaurant—the sort foolish mortals dine at when they wished to impress others—with white tablecloths, water sculpture in the lobby, and modern art on the walls. A young woman in black slacks and a crisp white blouse immediately moved to greet him then froze with a gaping mouth.

What is the matter? Never laid eyes on a lethal immortal assassin before?

"I'm meeting someone," he said. "She goes by the name of—" He slipped his phone from his pants pocket and toggled to Tommaso's text. It read: *Sorry, man. Something came up. Meet Samantha at eight o'clock at the Langosta Caliente.*

When he'd checked the address and found it was a restaurant in Santa Monica, he decided to get a room at the Beverly Hills—the presidential suite—so they would have easy access to a place to fuck. No, he did not believe for a moment that this Samantha was his mate; however, that did not signify he wouldn't permit her to suck his cock. Or sleep with him. *Maybe both.* Hell, if she bothered to go on a date with him, he owed her that much, didn't he? After all, he was a gentleman.

He looked at the terrified human hostess waiting for him to speak.

"Her name is Samantha," he said.

The female bobbed her head. "Oh. Yes. Uh…right this way, sir." The woman stumbled as she turned for the dining room.

Slow the hell down, woman. The hostess practically sprinted through the candlelit restaurant filled with well-dressed mortals oblivious to the fact that many still lived thanks to men like himself.

He took his time, his eyes carefully scanning the room for any threats—a habit he would never break—before reaching the table next to the window. He took one look at the blonde in the tight red dress who sat staring at him, and he knew; she wasn't his mate. He felt nothing.

So why had Cimil arranged this date, then? There had to be a reason, and with Cimil it was never straightforward or simple. A bigger plan was always at play.

Regardless, this female is hot. Pouty lips, big breasts, cute body. *All right. I will still allow her the pleasure of my cock.*

He grunted at the hostess, who scurried away as he sat. "You're Samantha?" he said.

The woman's jaw sort of hung open while she slowly bobbed her head.

Yes, I know. It's not every day you see six and half feet of such a fine male specimen sitting across from you. "I am Andrus."

She nodded stiffly.

Suddenly, he smelled fear. His head whipped over his shoulder, his eyes searching the room for danger.

Nothing.

When he moved his eyes back to the woman, he realized the smell came from her, and he laughed.

"Wha-what's so funny?" she said, her voice shaking.

"You. You're funny." He leaned in a bit, and she squeaked, shirking away. "No need to be afraid, Samantha. I have already decided to take you back to my hotel room after we dine. And if you're a good girl and eat your veggies, I'll make you scream." He winked. There should always be a reward for eating your greens. It was what the parenting handbook had said. Made sense to apply it to women, yes? They were similar to children. *Except Helena. She is a fearless vampire with the strength and fire of twenty warriors.*

Samantha's dull blue eyes—nowhere near as lovely as Helena's—widened in shock. She popped from her seat, turned, and ran straight out of the restaurant.

Andrus blinked while the other patrons did their best not to look at him. *Hell*—he scratched his stubbly jaw—*was it something I said?*

He cupped his hand over his mouth and took a whiff of his breath. *Whisky. Smells nice.* He shrugged, glad the date was over and that he could get back to his life of solitude.

He opened the menu sitting atop the table. *Hmm. Ceviche.*

Suddenly, he had a feeling deep in his gut. This wasn't over, was it? No, he felt something coming.

Something dark and evil. The strange part was, however, that feeling in his gut was a happy little tingle. Like whatever awaited him was a good thing.

He shook his head. *You're an idiot.* Nothing good ever awaited him. *Especially when Cimil is involved.*

It took Andrus most of the night to finally fall asleep. Something about the big quiet room, decorated with fine, khaki-colored, 1930s-style furniture (still very modern in his opinion), felt awkward. He also hadn't slept in a bed in a very long time. A) He didn't require much sleep, and B) he'd spent most nights snoozing with the Count— Matty's favorite stuffed doll from *Sesame Street*— in the armchair in Matty's room. The last time he actually recalled sleeping well was with Helena before she'd married Niccolo. Yes, yes, she had been his captive at the time, and no, nothing happened but for a bit of innocent spooning; however, it had been the most luxuriously sound sleep he could ever remember. However, now that he had peace and quiet—no evil vampires, restless baby vampires, or other threats to worry about— he found it difficult to relax.

Finally, after raiding the minibar and jerking off to some strange porn where two women took turns spanking each other, he closed his eyes and drifted off in the early morning only to be awoken by cold, wet liquid poured over his face.

"What the…" He jumped from the bed, swiping his machete from beneath his pillow. When his vision focused, he spotted a tall, large sonofabitch with long black hair and deep brown skin standing on the other side of the bed.

Roberto.

He had straps going every which way over his chest and arms and two prominent cloth sacks tethered to his torso. Chubby little coco-brown arms and legs stuck out from slits in the sacks.

"Very nice. Those the new Boba 4Gs?" Andrus asked, checking out the Cadillac of baby carriers.

"Organic cotton," Roberto replied, "with adjustable padded straps for both front," he twisted his large body to reveal two more babies strapped to his back, "or rear facing."

Excellent choice. Back support was important.

"So what brings you to my room so early in the morning?" Andrus was careful not to provoke a fight with this man. Not because he was the original vampire and strong as hell, but because Andrus had a no-unnecessary-fights rule when children were present.

"Cimil wanted to come herself, but when she foresaw that you would be sleeping nude, I wouldn't allow it." Roberto's eyes flashed down to Andrus's naked groin.

Andrus shrugged and then reached for his

leather pants, which were in a heap on the floor. "Sleeping in pajamas is for pansies."

"Sleep. I miss sleep." Roberto's dark eyes glazed over. "You get one down for a nap, and the other wakes. By the time you get that one settled, the first one is done napping. And it goes on...and on...and on." He sighed. "Why did Cimil's sister have to overdo it on the fertility spell?"

Akna, Goddess of Fertility, was one of the fourteen gods. It was said she was so powerful that one misdirected touch or look could get animals from entirely different species to go at it. The jackalope and tree octopus, for example? *Oh no, my friend. Those little buggers are real.* He'd seen them with his own eyes during his many years of travels.

"Try the white-noise machine for naptime," Andrus suggested, opening the khaki velveteen curtains to let in some depressing, smog-tinted sunlight. He liked his sunshine pre-industrial revolution. "I used it for Matty. Helped drown out the noise pollution of the city."

Roberto bobbed his head. "I most certainly will. Thank you."

"So, might I ask: Why the water in my face?"

Roberto gave him a cold stare. "Cimil made me promise to," he made air quotes with his fingers, "'throw a drink in the asshole's face.' She said it was for some woman named Samantha. Ring a bell?"

He rubbed his jaw. "I said two words to the female, and she fled." *Women. So infantile.* "And what the hell is Cimil up to anyway? That woman from last night was supposed to be my mate. As if I would ever be joined with a human." *They are so weak.* Of course, the options in the immortal world were very limited: Deities—all crazy; vampires—not many females; angels—too goodie, goodie; incubi and succubae—rare, if not extinct; demigods, like himself, also few and far between; Maaskab—evil Mayan priests—not into that; sex faeries, unicorns, and some others that were in no way "relationship" material.

"You must mistake me, demigod, for someone who cares," Roberto said dryly. "And now, if you do not mind, I must take your leave to buy a new evil puppy before my little ones awaken. We have apparently misplaced yet another. Or they ate it. We are unsure."

Andrus cringed. *Fuck.* Universe help them all. When those little bastards got big enough to walk, he could only imagine the death, destruction and mayhem they would rain down on the world. Cimil and Roberto's children would put the fear of the devil into Satan himself.

Roberto dug an envelope from one of the pockets on the front of the baby pouch and flung it on the bed. "That is for you. Perhaps the answers you seek are inside."

"Thanks, but I—"

"You will read it, or I will return later when the children are awake. With the children, of course."

Andrus blinked. "I'll read it. I promise." *Please don't come back.*

"Very good." Roberto glanced at the corner of the room. "Come, Minky. Let us hurry and procure a new plaything for my evil seeds." Roberto disappeared from the room, sifting to wherever ancient ex-pharaohs shopped for evil pets for evil children.

A shiver rolled through Andrus, realizing that Minky had just been in his room. *I hope they got rid of her fleas.* It was said that being bitten felt like getting stabbed with a knife. And they were invisible, too.

He walked over to the window with the view of a smog-coated L.A. and opened the letter. It was from Cimil, and it better fucking explain why he was here:

Dear King of Asshats,
Since you bombed big time with Samantha, as I knew you would because I know everything, I have already arranged for a second date tonight with Alexis. She is a nice girl who enjoys men with good hygiene and clothes that do not reek of death. She is also partial to men who do not threaten to take her to their hotel room to be murdered.

Murdered? He'd simply told the other woman, Samantha, that he would make her scream...*oh. Oops.* He supposed his looks and assassin-like vibe might have given the woman the wrong impression. He read on,

I strongly suggest, and by suggest, I mean you shall obey or suffer my wrath—I strongly suggest that you tidy yourself up and behave like a gentleman this evening.

Andrus scratched the back of his head, wondering what Cimil's endgame was. He had agreed to go on one date. One. With a woman who might be his second-chance mate. Now she wanted him to go on another? That had not been the deal.

He flipped over the page to read,

That is a good question, Andrus. The first date was merely a test, to see what we were up against. Holy clown-crap, you're a mess. This next date is your second opportunity to fine-tune your manly skills of wooing before our big immortal mixer bash in eight days. I've arranged to have your new mate be there, but you will have to work to win her over since her heart will not be automatically handed to you like the keys to dear old mom's castle.

She knows I have a castle? he thought, and continued reading,

Yes, I know about the castle. And about what's in the basement. Really? Really? And you call yourself a warrior? Any whoodles, don't fuck up this match. I have foreseen that Zac will flip out because he probably spends too much time in the mortal world. And flipped-out gods do evil things like destroy planets and pluck out eyeballs and gonads—specifically yours.

Andrus gave it a moment of thought. He didn't believe her little scare tactic about Zac, and he didn't want this. He didn't want love or a mate, now that he'd had a few days to think this all over. Nothing ever worked out well, and he was only setting himself up for disappointment. *No, thank you.*

Alrighty, if a deity losing his marbles, ripping off your manhood, and killing everything on the planet will not persuade you to get on the Cimi-train for a ride to everlasting love, then I would like to remind you of the following: Matty's happiness depends on your success. If you fail, she will never love as she is meant to. She will never be loved as she is meant to.

Andrus sat down on the plush bed, feeling like the wind had been knocked out of him. It had been a very long time since he'd thought about all that. How had he forgotten? *Probably because you try to ignore anything that comes out of Cimil's lying mouth?*

No, asshole. It wasn't a lie. As I told you long ago (in that other story you appear in) Matty is destined to grow up and marry your son, her mate. Unlike you, she will not be given a second chance. Have a fan-fucking-tastic date.

Sincerely,

Cimil, milk jugs for the spawn of mankind's destruction

Andrus crumpled up the letter and chucked it in the wastepaper basket across the enormous room.

"Sonofabitch!" How did he end up in these messes? Now he *had* to become mated in eight days. With his luck, the woman would be a heartless maniac like his first mate. And who the hell ever heard of having to "woo" a mate? Was this some perverse prank? Mates were your ideal. Your other cosmic half. The cream and sugar to your coffee. Of course, his mate history had been an exception to the rules to begin with. *Why stop now?*

He blew out a breath. *Fuck, fuck, fuck.*

He envisioned Matty's sweet little face and what a bright, intelligent woman she would grow up to be. Then he imagined her withering away on the vine, without anyone to love for eternity.

He shook his head. *Very well. I will do my practice date tonight and woo away.*

The question was, did he really know how?

CHAPTER FOUR

"No. No. No. I'm going to lose my apartment?" Twenty-three-year-old Sadie Townsend looked at the eviction notice in her hand and sighed. She had exactly fifteen days to pay the rent or she'd be thrown out of her closet, aka studio apartment the size of a steam trunk with horrible brown shag carpet and 1970s pea-green kitchenette.

What am I going to do?

She didn't want to go crawling back to her parents in Cleveland, where she would be forced to endure the endless stream of lectures. *Why didn't you finish college? When will you grow up and get a real job that pays the bills? Why can't you stay in Cleveland and pursue your career?*

Because actors didn't make careers in Cleveland. They moved to L.A. or New York.

She scrubbed her face with two hands and groaned. She could probably pick up a few more shifts between the two restaurants she worked at, but it wouldn't be enough. She'd have to work double-time, including day shifts, but if she did that, she wouldn't have time for the auditions that she just knew were coming. Signing up for a shift and not showing wasn't an option, either. It would cost her the job completely.

She stared at the notice and ran her hand over the top of her head, twisting her long ponytail in her hand. *There have to be some G-rated ways to make a couple thousand.* All she needed was to make it another month or two. She'd gone on four casting calls recently, all for speaking parts in different movies where she was a perfect fit both for the personality of the roles and the physical description—fair complexion, medium build, auburn hair, and brown eyes. *I'm so close to something big. I can feel it.*

Her phone rang and she jumped. It was buried somewhere in her bed. She threw the floral sheets and blankets to the floor, following the sound.

"There you are, you little shit." She looked at the screen and felt her hopes fizzle. "Hi, Carlos." She listened to the owner of the restaurant she worked at. "Yeah, I can come in early tonight." She listened. "And stay late. Thanks." What the hell. Extra hours were extra hours.

She hung up and went into her postage-stamp-sized bathroom, with old cigarette stains on the '70s-orange tub and sink, to get ready for work. Either she got a good-paying job acting or she'd be homeless.

And done with L.A.

Sadly, her friends slash acquaintances weren't in much better shape. Most of them—okay, all of them—were struggling actors, too. Four or five guys or girls sharing a small apartment. Then there was the reality that many couldn't be depended on for help anyway. A lot of the folks she met at work or in her acting group would up and leave L.A., never to be heard from again. She supposed it was the reality of pursuing a career in Hollywood. Many couldn't take the rejections.

I could reconsider Tim's offer. He'd asked her to move in with him, but they just hadn't known each other very long. Two months. On the other hand, he was a nice steady guy who owned a gallery over in Malibu—exactly the kind of man she should date. They'd met when she'd been hired to serve wine at one of the gallery's big openings. And when she said "big opening," she meant it. Vaginas everywhere. A huge walk-through vagina sculpture that was supposed to give the feeling of being born, talking robotic vaginas sitting on a sofa and discussing Plato on a hidden speaker loop, and vagina beanbag chairs. There were so many vaginas, she'd wondered if that was what it felt like to be a player's penis. When she actually shared the thought out loud, the man next to her started to laugh.

"Welcome to my world," he'd said.

"Oh. So you're a big dick, huh?"

"I feel like it for having this show in my gallery—the artist is a friend of mine."

"He must really be into women." She chuckled.

"No. Just their vaginas," he replied. "Ironic, because my friend is gay."

"Well, that sounds like the making of a good psychiatry patient."

He laughed, and before she left, he asked for her number, which thrilled her. The man was positively beautiful—dark eyes, dark skin, lean and muscular. Around date number four, after he'd given her a very strange evening of sex where he kept telling her to eat him up, he asked her to move in. Regardless of the strange pillow talk, she wasn't ready. And oddly, every time she started to have second thoughts about dating him, he'd show up at her work or at her door. Then he'd kiss her, and she'd feel all tingly and into him again. It was strange. So strange.

No. You are definitely not moving in with that guy. In fact, she needed to dump Tim, now that she thought about it. She didn't quite feel safe around him. *After work. I'll do it after work.* Yes, it was the right choice. She needed her life cleared of any distractions so she could focus on two things: getting a job to save her apartment and not losing faith in her dream.

Easier said than done. She didn't know how much more of the pressure and rejections she could take.

Don't think that way. You can figure this out, Sadie. Just have faith.

☙❧

Later that evening, a few hours into her shift at the *churrascaria*, or Brazilian steak house, three of the *passadores*, or "meat servers," decided not to show for the dinner rush shift.

Real nice, guys. Strangely, not a one had mentioned that they'd be ditching work when everyone went for drinks after closing last night. *Probably decided to drive to Baja.* The three boneheads were roomies, notorious flakes, and big-time surfers.

I don't know who's worse, surfers or actors. This was the fifth time something like this had happened since she started working there a few months ago. But they'd never had three no-shows in one night.

Carlos, the owner, who was a middle-aged man with a fake tan and a bald head, shoved a thick leather belt with attached carving knife at her. "You will have to cover for them, Sadie. Go put on your costume." Being from Brazil, he had a thick accent and conveniently forgot how to speak English whenever anyone tried to tell him no. Not that she was in a position to refuse him, but it might make sense to point out the obvious.

"Carlos, you've never trained me to work with those knives. Do you really want me bleeding all over the customers?" She was a regular waitress, the one who served wine, side dishes, and anything else that was not meat roasted on a giant skewer and then sliced off in little strips right at the table.

It required a steady hand used to working with a sharp knife and the ability to balance what was basically a sizzling hot sword stacked with meat in the other.

"You are an actress," Carlos said, "so act." He headed into the back office to start calling every waitperson on the roster, but it was Friday night in L.A. He wouldn't get anyone. That meant she and the two other waiters would have to cover the entire restaurant on the busiest damned night of the week. Not that the place was huge—about twenty-five tables total—but they were going to be swamped.

I hope the guests are into finger food, 'cause one of them will be getting mine on their plate tonight. She headed to the kitchen locker room to find a costume and put on her *passador* belt.

Ten minutes later, she emerged into the dining room, tucking her white blouse into her black gaucho pants—kind of like capris with some serious flare. She'd tied up her long brown hair into a tight bun for safety reasons, and then used a red scarf to hide the scratch marks on her neck. She'd been waking up with them all over her body lately, the results of stress and nightmares, she guessed.

She turned the corner and slammed right into something warm that smelled like sinful manly deliciousness—leather and freshly cut wood and some other floral notes she couldn't pinpoint.

When her gaze traveled up, up, up, two bright

turquoise-blue eyes stared down at her with amusement.

"Oh God," she said. "I'm so sorry." She jerked her hands back from the man and watched a devilish smile form on his two sexy lips. With the short black beard he sported, his mouth looked like a sexual centerpiece, created for serious adoration.

"No worries," he said, with a slightly accented voice as deep as the ocean and as silky as her black panties.

Panties? What panties? Hers had just melted off.

Sadie tried to pull her eyes away, but looking at his face was addictive. *He's so goddamned beautiful.* Slightly high cheekbones, square jaw, straight nose with a faded scar across the bridge. That short dark hair was kind of a mess, like he'd just showered and dried it with a towel, but the rest of him looked like sleek sex in a dark suit—tall, lean, and muscular, with an air of old-world sophistication. Or maybe not sophistication as much as it was...well, she couldn't put her finger on it.

"Eh-hem," a woman nearby cleared her throat, knocking Sadie back to reality.

Reluctantly, Sadie peeled her eyes from the gorgeous, tall, godlike man and found a slender brunette with long hair, bulgy eyes—sort of like a reptile might have—wearing a skimpy black dress, and hanging on his arm.

How embarrassing. She'd totally been caught drooling over this woman's date.

"Can we be seated now?" the woman said in a bitchy tone.

"Oh. Uh..." Sadie looked around the crowded restaurant. The hostess was busy serving water. Everyone was doing three jobs tonight. "Right this way."

She turned to show them to a table and caught the man not so subtly looking her over and smirking. *Thanks, buddy. Like the outfit? Just wait until you see me with the sword*. It would only get better.

As she weaved through the tables, she tried not to pay too much attention to the tower of hot man oozing sex and raw male virility behind her. But something about the way he carried himself made it hard not to sneak a few peeks. He wore a very expensive-looking suit over that muscular frame, but he definitely didn't act like some nouveau riche, superficial Beverly Hills douche bag that were a dime a dozen in this city. This guy even smelled different. And he definitely made her womanly bits perk up their little ears like a pack of tiny crotch wolves who scented something delicious in the air.

Crotch wolves? Seriously, Sadie.

"Here you go." She gestured toward the small empty table, trying her best not to make eye contact with the man and his smoldering turquoise gaze.

The woman's face twisted with disgust. "I'm not sitting there. It's too close to the kitchen. It's all smoky."

It wasn't smoky, but Sadie didn't want to argue with a customer, and after drooling over the woman's date, she kind of felt bad, too.

"Not a problem," Sadie said, "uh…" *Crap!* The only other table was across the restaurant in her section. *Just great. Now I have to try not to drool on the guy while I serve his food.* "Right this way."

While she walked them to the table, she felt his eyes on her the entire time, the air between them growing sexually electric. Or was she imagining it?

"I'll be right back with menus," Sadie said nervously, once they reached the empty table in the corner. As she turned away, she noticed the reptile-eyed woman waiting for the huge, magnificent man to pull out her chair. Instead, he sat himself down, continuing to keep his eyes locked hungrily on Sadie.

Oh, my god. That man is so hot. And he so should not be looking at me. Just like she should not be looking at him. The customer. On a date with a woman.

When Sadie returned with menus, the woman was snarling at her date, who seemed too occupied to give a crap, his cold, fierce gaze scanning the restaurant almost like he sensed some sort of threat. It instantly put her on edge.

"Here are your menus," Sadie said. "Have either

of you had *churrascaria* before?" Sadie clasped her hands together to keep them from trembling.

The man looked up at her with those shockingly icy blue-green eyes, which he then slid down her body, slowly sweeping her from head to toe before settling on her breasts for a few seconds too long.

"Yes," he finally replied, in a deep sensual voice laced with an ominous vibe. "However, I like the sound of your voice. Continue talking."

Thinking he'd made a joke, Sadie laughed anxiously.

He didn't laugh with her. "Do I amuse you, woman?"

She blinked. Had he really called her "woman," like some medieval barbarian? "Uh, no sir. Sorry, sir. I was just thinking of a joke someone told me earlier."

He gave a cool nod. "Go on."

"Oh, yes. Well, we serve the meat here straight from the kitchen's fire pit, right at your table. If you prefer, however, we also have menu items—a selection of vegetarian or fish entrees. The side dishes are also listed there. May I start you off with a salad?"

He flashed her a stern look. "I meant the joke. I want to hear what is so damned funny."

"Andrus," his date snapped, "let the woman get back to work."

His name was Andrus. Funny how it suited him—strong, classic, masculine. *With a pinch of jerk.*

He slowly peeled his eyes off of Sadie and moved them to his date. "Silence, Alexis."

Oh. Make that a side helping of jerk. She never would put up with that kind of crap from a man no matter how hot and mysterious. On the other hand, something about this guy screamed dark and dangerous, like the sort of guy you should stay away from if you valued your life.

"Umm...I'll be back with those salads." Sadie scurried away, feeling the man's eyes locked onto her until she reached the sanctuary of the kitchen, where she let out a long breath and tried to calm her heart. He literally made her quake in her sensible black flats. At the same time, he was so beautiful, looking at him provoked this gnawing need to look again.

I definitely shouldn't be serving that guy.

She quickly went to work making ten plates of salads for several tables and laying them out on a huge tray while the other waiters rushed in and out. She grabbed Steve, a sandy blond preppy type, as he headed for the drink machine.

"Hey, can you switch sections with me?" she asked.

"No way, man. I have a party of ten and the tip is mandatory."

Dammit. She didn't want to wait on Mr. Hottie

and his date, Snapping Turtle.

She took a quick breath, propped the tray on her shoulder, and set out to the dining room. When she left the salads for the giant, scary, sexy, rude man, he and his date were thankfully busy bickering. Something about demigods being bigger badasses than vampires.

Okay. Weird convo. Keep moving.

After the salads were out, she made the rounds with bar drinks and water. When she got to the last table, her heart made a little flip. The man was staring at her with that hard, sensual gaze. And now he sat alone.

She tried to smile politely, but her mouth didn't want to seem to go in that direction. "Do you know what your date would like to drink, si-si-sir?" Her hand shook violently as she reached to fill his water glass.

He snagged her wrist. "Who are you?" he asked, but his tone felt like more of an accusation.

She froze with the glass in her trembling hand, the pitcher of water in the other. "I'm s-sorry?" she stuttered.

His thumb made soft little circles on the inside of her wrist. "Why are you shaking?"

"Let me go," she whispered, liking the feel of his touch way more than she should.

He grinned devilishly and dipped his head, his eyes never leaving her face. "As you like. But tell me your name first."

"Sadie," she said.

He released her, leaving behind sharp little tingles over her wrist. She slapped her hand over the spot.

"Andrus," said the man's date, returning to the table, her big eyes twitching with anger, "did you order my wine?"

Still staring at Sadie, his grin grew large and cocky. "I would like two fingers of whatever sad excuse for scotch your bar stocks, and please bring my *date* a glass of Merlot. Thank you, Sadie." Her name rolled off his tongue like a sexual innuendo.

Dear Lord. What is it with this guy? The way he looked at her made her want to get naked with him. And run away. *So weird.*

"Be right back." She went to the bar toward the front of the restaurant, placed their order, and grabbed a glass filled with ice water to roll across her forehead. She'd never in her life felt like this before. *But this guy...this guy...fuck, he's scary hot. And just plain scary.*

How would she make it through the rest of his meal?

A few minutes later, it was time to make the rounds with the first meat course: sirloin steaks that were folded onto a long hot skewer for cooking, and then sliced thinly at the table right onto the customer's plate.

She'd seen it done many times, but had never served the dish herself.

Shit. With her right hand, she tried to grip both the handle of the sharp knife and the top of the piping-hot, three-foot-long skewer while trying to hold on to the slippery metal juice tray in the other hand.

Once situated, she headed out of the kitchen and stopped. *Dammit.* The *passadores* were supposed to start at the far end of the room and work their way back toward the kitchen. *Fuck.* That meant serving the gorgeous, scary man first.

She awkwardly maneuvered the gargantuan kabob and made her way over, almost dropping the entire thing on the floor twice.

"Would you care for some steak?" she asked, approaching the table, trying her best to smile. The man caught a glimpse of her and sprang from his seat in a blur. She fell back, her meat skewer and knife going only God knew where, and landed on the tile floor with a hard thump, knocking the wind from her.

The crazy man pressed her arms above her head to the floor, his entire body covering hers. "What is the fucking meaning of this?" he growled in her face. "Who are you?"

Gasping for air, her body crushed under his weight, she tried to scream but couldn't. Or didn't want to. His warmth and hardness on top of her momentarily vanquished all thoughts of reason from her mind. The only thing that seemed to matter was the sensation of his body nestled between her legs, his hip bone—or something hard—pressing right into her, coaxing all sorts of tingles and sexual aches.

Commotion erupted in the restaurant, snapping Sadie back into awareness that she was lying on the restaurant floor underneath this large man, who was actually assaulting her.

"You think you can take me down with a little knife?" he snarled.

"Dammit, Andrus. You barbaric asshole," barked the man's date, "she was not trying to attack you, she was trying to serve you meat."

A moment passed as the man stared into her eyes, still lying right on top of her, his cock nestled right up against her crotch. She felt his heart pounding away in his chest, the rhythm strangely matching her own frantic beats, like two war drums pounding together.

Ohmygod. What am I doing enjoying this?

You are not. You're offended!

Yes. I am.

His eyes moved to her lips and then a cocky, devious smile worked onto his mouth. "Whoops. Guess I overreacted," he said in a slow, deep unabashed voice.

He thought this was funny? He'd knocked the wind out of her and everyone was staring while she'd experienced an embarrassingly erotic moment that proved she was nuts or completely hard up for a man. *Or into having public sex.*

"Fucking asshole," she snarled, catching her air, "get off."

A wicked little smile flickered across his lips. "Perhaps later," he whispered. "At present, I'm on a date."

"Gah!" She pushed him back.

He rose to his feet and held out his hand while his eyes gave her a smug, knowing look. He knew exactly what had just happened to her: She'd liked it.

She glanced at his hand and that amused smile and lost it. "Take that hand and shove it up your ass."

"Sadie!" Carlos appeared in a gaucho outfit. "What is going on?"

Sadie got up off the floor and pointed at Andrus. "This man just attacked me."

Andrus nodded. "Yes. However, it was just a simple misunderstanding. I suffer from PTSD or whatever you people call it these days." He shrugged.

Carlos looked up at the hulking man. "Sir, my apologies. I assure you this is not the manner we treat war veterans. I will deal with her."

"What? This jackass just threw me on the floor," Sadie barked.

Carlos shot her a look. "Kitchen now."

Andrus interceded. "I assure you, I am fine. No need to scold the tiny meat wench."

"Meat wench? Someone needs to beat some

manners into you."

Smirking, the man raised one dark brow and then glanced at his groin. "You may *beat* me anytime you like."

He did not just insinuate I jerk him off. Where the hell was that knife? "You disgusting pig!"

"Sadie, get out of my restaurant. Immediately," Carlos seethed.

She held up her hands. "Fine. No problem." She looked right up at Andrus. "If I ever see you again," she growled, "I'll remove your nut sack with my teeth." *Wait. That came out all wrong.* Why would she want to put her teeth down there? "I meant...with a butter knife." Yeah, that sounded more painful. But would also require her to really hold on to those bad boys while she tried to saw them off. *Ick.* "Or something sharp. I'm not sure."

The man grinned, clearly enjoying her lame attempt to threaten him.

She shushed him as he was about to speak and left the restaurant. *Great. Fucking great. He tries to murder me, and I get fired.* Still, a part of her wanted to go back there, tear off his clothes, and kiss the hell out of him. *And then kill him.* Because now she'd lost her job. She'd never make up what she owed on the rent.

I'm going to have to do something drastic. But what?

CHAPTER FIVE

"All right, big boy. I am officially declaring you a dating crime scene." Standing over Andrus's bed, a pair of wide turquoise eyes glared down at him.

"Ugh," he grumbled and rolled onto his stomach. "Go away, Cimil."

"Ha!" she laughed. "I will pretend that you didn't just say that because we both know you didn't mean it. Just like the time you said you didn't want to see me naked, but I knew you did."

Dear gods, please make her leave. He had a raging hangover—two bottles of whisky last night, which was what it took to get drunk given how quickly his body metabolized the alcohol.

"I need sleep, Cimil. And that time you forced me to see you nude left me scarred for months."

He felt something wet and cold slither across the bottom of his foot. "Holy fuck!" He jumped from the bed, his head whipping from side to side.

Cimil grinned. "Just be glad you're wearing pants. Minky loves to eat anything that looks like a hot dog."

He glared at her. "Hot dog? I assure you my penis resembles more of a fine Russian kolbasa." Yes. The Russians, now they knew how to make cured meats. Just like they knew how to make fearless warriors, like himself. His family had been from St. Petersburg originally, although he'd been living in Paris, attending yet another boring ball, when he'd met Reyna, the queen of vampires and his mate. She'd robbed him of everything he once was, and now all that remained from his past was his iron will.

Andrus noticed Cimil staring hungrily at his crotch. *Dear gods, no.* "Cimil, you are married now. And even if you weren't—"

"Oh, you think you get a say, do you?" She talked right at his groin. "You think you can boss me around? I am a deity!"

"I am not bossing you around. I'm asserting my free will. You may not have your way with me."

"Careful. Or I'll shove my fist right down that little hole."

Dear fucking gods. He stepped back, but Cimil's eyes remained focused on the spot she'd been looking at, not on his crotch.

Thank gods. She was merely having one of her episodes. He did not want to think about the years of therapy he'd require if she molested him.

"Cimil?" He snapped his fingers. "Who are you speaking to?"

Nothing.

"Cimil!" He clapped loudly.

"Wow!" She shook her head from side to side. "Those leprechauns are intense! All that shiny gold." She sighed. "So where were we?"

"You were leaving."

"Great. So it's all settled, then. Since I've now demonstrated you can't do this woo-wooing on your own, and I can't afford to let you fail, you will graciously agree to work with the tutor I've hired. She's got just the right personality to help you connect with your inner Prince Charming, and she's seen you in action. Your classes begin tomorrow at nine in the morning. She will be here at ten."

Seen me in action? So that's really what these warm-up dates were about. Cimil was having some sort of "charm school" teacher secretly evaluate him.

"What exactly do you think this woman can teach me that I don't already know?" he asked. "And why would classes begin before the instructor arrives?"

Cimil held up her finger and began sliding her other hand over it in an obscene gesture. "You'll be wanting a little me time with your kolbasa beforehand because your teacher is very, very hot. So if you don't prepare properly, you won't be able to concentrate. Did I not already say that?" she replied.

He growled. "No. You didn't. And I'm not doing this. Whatever godsdamned bullshit you've got going, I won't be a part of it."

She wagged her finger. "Uh-uh-uh...Remember poor little Matty. Your future baby-mama is going to be at that mixer, and if you don't get her to kiss you before she leaves, the window will close. Poof. And then you won't knock her up, won't live happily ever after, Matty won't find happiness, and you'll end up spanking the Russian salami on your own for eternity. Or until Minky eats you. Or Zac flips out and kills every living creature on the planet. Whichever comes first."

This was preposterous. "I do not need a teacher. Women like me just fine."

"We're not talking about those women; we're talking about one in particular who you can't afford to fuck up with: your mate Charlotte."

Her name was Charlotte. Suddenly, knowing her name made everything feel a bit more real. *But not entirely.*

Cimil continued, "And your teacher is really an actress. She's going to teach you to *act* like a gentleman since we already know you can't be one."

"I am a warrior, a trained assassin, an ex-Demilord—"

"You're an out-of-work manny, and your assassin days are over. There are no more evil vampires." She took a bow. "Thanks to my evil mastery, they've been wiped out. And the Maaskab are pretty much extinct. We left a few around just for shits and giggles. That leaves us only with humans and their dredge of society, which is not your problem, that's the domain of the gods. So the way I see it, Andrus baby, you. Are. Officially.

Retired. Your only remaining purpose is to make the mate plunge."

Andrus blinked at Cimil, feeling like his entire world had been ripped away. She was right. Up until recently, the world had been filled with evil and on an imminent path to destruction. How Cimil pulled it all off was a mystery, or a miracle, but she'd managed to convince her mate, Roberto, to hunt down and kill his evil brother, thereby eliminating that bloodline and all evil vampires. The Maaskab, who'd allied themselves with Roberto's brother, some becoming vampires, too, were mostly killed off.

He took a breath. "I-I-I have no purpose. I'm...obsolete."

Cimil stuck out her lower lip. "Now, now. Don't get all pouty on me. If we're all still alive, I'm sure there will be another outbreak of evil immortal villains in a few thousand years. Then we'll dust you off or ask Minky to burp you out."

He felt like crying. Not that big, lethal immortal men like him actually cried, but he sure as hell felt like doing it anyway.

"Please leave," he said.

"But—"

"Out, Cimil!" he barked.

"Jeez. Fine. I'm leaving," she said petulantly. "But don't forget your teacher's coming tomorrow."

"Yeah. Whatever." At this moment, he didn't

give a fuck about any of that. He'd been so wrapped up caring for and protecting little Matty, he'd not seen that his purpose no longer existed.

"I gotta go now anyway. Time to water the children." She headed for the door. "And BTW, the instructor is mortal and thinks you're an actor and that I am Bob, her agent. Tootles." Cimil closed the door behind her.

Marvelous. Fucking marvelous. Mortals were on a need-to-know basis only. That meant she couldn't know what he was. For the record, he'd crossed that line where hiding his immortality from humans wasn't easy. He'd spent far too many years embracing who he was—*which you no longer are*—so obeying the unwritten rule of lying low was like asking a monkey not to pick its fleas.

He sat on the edge of his bed and covered his face, not knowing if he had it in him to exist if the only thing he had to look forward to was his mate, who would likely ruin him.

"I can't believe it. I'm a relic. Obsolete. Useless."

Just because your life sucks doesn't mean you have to ruin Matty's.

He groaned and then felt something wet and cold slide across his cheek. "Fuck. Cimil!" he screamed. "Take your fucking unicorn with you!"

She popped through the door, reached for something, and then headed out. "Oops," she mumbled as she disappeared. "Sorry about that. Thought Minky was with me."

CHAPTER SIX

Sadie could not believe her luck. Just when she thought she'd have to choose between heading home or becoming a stripper to make ends meet, she'd gotten a call from her agent, Bob.

"They want to pay me how much?" she asked him, standing in her bedroom slash living room slash kitchen, stirring her mug of instant coffee—complete crap, but the only thing she could afford. These days, dollar-store cuisine was on the menu. It was either that or not having enough money for gas. Thankfully, her car was paid for.

"One hundred thousand." Bob chuckled like the slimeball that he was. "Minus my twenty percent, of course."

Ugh. Bob had been the only talent agent willing to take her on in a town where aspiring actresses were a dime a dozen, and he gave her the jeepers creepers. Meaning, she sometimes had the feeling he was seriously evil. Why were all of the men she met in L.A. rich, superficial assholes, self-centered actors, or authentic stand-ins for Hannibal Lector?

"Seriously? One hundred? Which movie?" She'd auditioned for the new paranormal shifters remake of *Gone with the Wind* called *Gone Without End—a Southern Tail of Immortal Love*; part two of *Fifty*

Shades of Zombie called *Fifty-One Shades of Grrraaay*; and the slam-dunk blockbuster *Double-Oh-Merman*—kind of a James Bond meets Poseidon, but with these really mean mermen as the villains. Apparently, the paranormal theme was making a huge Hollywood comeback after a hiatus attributed to *Twilight* market saturation. But her agent assured her that these were A-list movies.

"Yeah, Sippy," Bob replied. "That's the thing. It's not a movie as much as it is...a coaching gig."

Why in the world Bob insisted on calling her "Sippy" she'd never know, but it was so damned annoying.

"Sorry? What do you mean by coaching?" she asked.

"The studio needs you to teach the star actor—who's been hailed as the next Thor—how to act like a gentleman. He's got one week until the shoot starts."

Whoa. They wanted her to train an actor? She supposed it made sense, considering she had years of acting lessons and had won a ton of awards for the small stage productions she'd done back home before deciding to come to L.A. She was definitely a solid actress, but also a very unlucky one. It seemed like every time she had a sure thing in the palm of her hand, disaster would strike—the film's financing would fall through at the last minute, the studio would decide to shift gears, or—as was the case in the last part she'd been sure of—the casting director went missing. Poof.

"Who am I going to coach? Gerard? Leo? Jack?" she asked.

"Well…"

Oh no. "This isn't some porn, is it? I told you no dick flicks, Bob!"

"No, Sippy baby. No. The guy is just a little rough around the edges. Needs a charm-school lesson, so he'll appeal to that whole rom-com crowd. You know."

Well, it was a lot of money, and if that was the job, who was she to complain? "Okay. No problem. But is there any chance I'll get a part in the movie?"

"Meh. Probably not," Bob replied.

That was disappointing, but this was the kind of money that would keep her afloat for at least another year.

"Done," she said. It would be a little tight having only one day to prepare, but she'd make it work. She had years of notes, books, binders, and CDs about acting as well as every acting exercise under the sun. It wouldn't take long to dig through it all and come up with a few lessons.

"Ah now, there's my girl. I'll shoot you the details and the contract."

That was odd. "What kind of contract?"

"Details, Sippy. Details."

"Bob?" she said, warning him with her voice. "What aren't you telling me?"

"Meh. Well…obviously ya can't blab to anyone

about the man. He's considered an up-and-comer. Studio wants to protect his public image."

That was fine. Actors got very touchy about public perception, and calling in another actor, especially someone unknown, to help prep for a part could be seen as a bit lame.

"And...?" she asked.

"Well...it seems the guy has a final audition, more like a check-in, in one week. If he doesn't get the thumbs-up, the role goes to their second choice and you don't get paid."

"What?" she barked.

"Hey, babe, acting is like a garage sale. I don't make the signs, I just follow them."

What a weird thing to say.

She nibbled her thumbnail, giving it some thought. This was a bit of a risk in that she could end up not getting paid. However, being an actress was her dream, and the way things stood, she'd be out on her butt in less than two weeks, heading back to Cleveland. *Or begging people to let me crash on their couches, like a total loser.* Which was more of a Band-Aid, leading back to Cleveland, not a solution. Tim wasn't an option either because they were through; although, she remembered trying to call and tell him she didn't want to see him anymore, but couldn't remember what happened. Had she left a message or spoken to him? It was the weirdest damned thing.

I guess I was too pumped up and pissed off last

night. That scene in the restaurant had been sheer insanity. The final insult being that she'd dreamed of that stupid man all night. Dirty, dirty dreams, too.

She thanked Bob and got the address of the hotel where she was supposed to meet her mystery student the next morning.

She then called her parents for their weekly chat. It was the one thing her father, the most protective guy on the planet, made her swear to do: call him once a week. Her mother—or stepmom, really, but Sadie thought of her like her real mother—was a super laid-back professor who taught mythology at the local J.C.

"Is that my little girl?" her father said, answering the phone.

"Yes, Daddy. Just calling to check in."

"Any news this week?"

I got fired? "Nothing yet. But soon. I went on four auditions and a few casting calls, too. I'm close, I can feel it."

"Baby, you've been in L.A. for over a year. Maybe it's time to come home."

He said the same thing every week.

"Dad, I can't leave now. I signed up to help this other actor, and if he gets the part, I get one hundred thousand dollars."

"Bob get you this gig?" he asked judgmentally.

"Of course. He's my agent."

"Uh-huh. Well, you be careful. This Bob person

can't be trusted."

"Dad, you don't even know him." Of course, her father was right.

"Yes, I do."

"Oh really? How?" she asked skeptically.

"I meant, I know his type. And he's only looking for a way to exploit you for his own gain."

"That's what he gets paid for, Dad. Hey, I gotta go. But say hi to Mom and Nell." Nell was her twenty-year-old sister.

"I will. Do you need me to send you any money?"

I'm so broke I've been washing my clothes with Dawn in the sink for a month. "I'm good, Dad. Thanks for offering."

"Okay. I just don't want you going hungry. You're not hungry, are you? Because you could tell me if you were."

She was an actress. She was always hungry. Especially lately. *I think I need to start taking vitamins.* "I promise if I need anything, I'll let you know, Dad. I love you."

"I love you, too, baby. And make sure to keep up with your brushing. Break a leg."

Her father was a dentist and crazy obsessed with having a clean mouth. "Thanks, Dad." She hung up and sighed. It was great how her father cared about her, but he worried too much.

Better than the alternative, I suppose. She could be one of those people who had nobody. God knew there were plenty of those in this city, which was a good reminder to always feel grateful for what she had.

But dammit, I want more. Which meant she'd need this guy to nail his part.

I wonder who he is.

⊱⊰

That next morning, at a quarter to ten, Sadie showed up with backpack in hand to the presidential suite at the Beverly Hills Hotel, ready to start teaching—body language, eye contact, conversation styles—but no one came to the door.

Standing in the hallway and wondering if she had the right room, she slipped her cell from her pocket and dialed Bob, but there was no answer. *Dang it.* Maybe she could call the room from down in the lobby.

She was about to leave when she heard a groan just inside the room. *Someone's in there.*

"Hey." Knock, knock. "I'm here for your coaching lesson. You okay?"

She pressed her ear to the door.

Groan.

The sound was deep and throaty, almost like the sound of a man...well, getting off.

She cupped her hands over her mouth. *I can't believe this guy.* The clock was ticking and it was really rude to keep someone waiting so he could wank it.

She gave the door another hard knock. "Listen, buddy, if you're doing anything but dying, you'd better open this door, or I'm leaving. And I'm pretty sure you don't want that."

The man groaned again, but this time the sound was so deep and hard, it sent shivers up her spine and down to her nether region. His voice was just so damned sexy.

What? Sadie, what's wrong with you?

"Oh. Come on, buddy!" Knock. Knock. Knock. "Can't you do that later?"

She suddenly heard some rustling and then the sound of something large thumping on the floor. The door flew open and a huge man, wearing partially unzipped leather pants, stood panting in the doorway, no underwear, his pants barely holding to his hips and slung low on his muscular torso. She could see a dark patch of hair and the base of his cock, which looked hard as hell, straining against the inside of his pants.

She gulped. The man was hung.

Her eyes moved up over the snug fabric of his black T-shirt, the muscles of his chest and arms stretching it to its limits. She was sure this guy was some sort of weight lifter or martial arts enthusiast. *Or the next Thor.* Just like Bob had said.

When her eyes finally got to his face, two intense turquoise eyes burned right through her, stopping her breath for several heartbeats until her brain registered the fact that it was the same face who'd visited her the last two evenings in two unwelcome, very erotic dreams.

"So we meet again, meat wench." His sinful lips flashed a smug little smile. "Why am I not surprised to see you here begging for more?"

Sadie blinked. "Holy crap. You're the crazy asshole from the other night." What were the odds? She took a step back, ready to run for the hills when it hit her. "Wait. You're an actor? You told Carlos you were a veteran!" She stepped forward and punched him right in his very broad shoulder.

"Ow," he winced, rubbing the spot.

"You asshole! I got fired because of you! Did it not occur to you to do your method acting elsewhere?"

The man—*What was his name? Oh, yeah. Andrus*—Andrus folded his giant cannons over his chest that reminded her of the hard, round cement bags in her mother's garden used to create a little pond for holding rainwater. It was her favorite place to play as a child.

"I am not an ex-soldier," he said insolently, "I am an ex-assassin. A lethal one."

Oh, God. This guy is going to stay in character the entire time. But at least it explained his weird, archaic behavior.

He added, "And has it ever occurred to you not

to run at strangers with carving knives? An invitation for a fight, if I ever saw one. But perhaps you're the sort who enjoys getting rough." His gaze moved down to her breasts, and she found herself wishing she'd worn something baggy instead of her white short-shorts and pink tank top. But she'd wanted to be comfortable while they did their warm-ups and role-playing.

"I-I-I do not enjoy getting rough," she replied, trying to pretend that his sexual undertones hadn't affected her. "And has it ever occurred to you not to go to a *churrascaria* restaurant if you—or your character—whatever—are touchy about knives? Seriously. And couldn't you have at least tried to tell my boss it was your fault?"

"Why would I falsely admit culpability? Nevertheless, I attempted to convey to the little man that I wasn't hurt or upset. I mean," he laughed, "look at you. You're harmless."

Sadie wanted to kick the man in his beautiful face, but it was way, way up there. The guy was like six six or something.

"Whatever. Are you ready to start your lesson, or do you need another decade to finish your weenie yoga?" Her eyes moved down to the X-rated view of his still semi-aroused cock, the base still very visible through the open fly.

And dammit if there wasn't something about his shamelessly unapologetic raw male sexuality that didn't make her want to keep looking.

He glanced down at his crotch. "You're fifteen minutes early; however, I think the moment has fled me. Some yappy little meat wench insisted on knocking down the door for a look." He cracked a snide little smile. "But feel free to take matters into your own hands. I trust you know how to handle *this* kind of sword at least?"

She grimaced in disgust. "No wonder you need my help. You're absolutely disgusting." *And I really need to stop looking at his huge penis.* "And your junk is far too tiny to interest my hands or any other part of my body."

He narrowed his smoldering, turquoise eyes. "And you are too small, insignificant, and plain to ever interest me. Don't ever forget that."

He did not just call me plain. Sadly, it sort of stung a little. No woman wanted to be called plain, especially by a beautiful asshole like this. *Don't let him shame you, Sadie. Just do the job, get paid, and get on with your life.*

On the other hand…

She stepped toward him, staring deeply into his eyes, and then reached out her hand, placing it firmly over the enormous sideways-slanted bulge in his leather pants.

She watched as his face and body tensed up. He probably thought she was going to assault his manhood. When she didn't, she could see that twinkle of hard lust in his eyes.

She leaned in and rubbed her breasts and body

against him like a frisky little sex kitten. His chest expanded with a few short, hard breaths. *Oh, yeah, big boy. I know how to act, too.*

"Plain, huh?" she whispered, standing on her tiptoes like she was going to go in for a kiss. The moment his head started to lower toward her, she slid both hands slowly to his open fly and zipped him up. "Put your teeny weeny away, Mr. Ass-Sasin," she pushed past him, "and let's get to work."

"That was a dirty trick, woman," he snarled. "And you could've injured some very sensitive equipment with the zipper."

"Yep. But I didn't." She entered the room, attempting to find a place for them to sit and begin going over the basics: table decorum, language, how to make a woman feel at ease. And from what she saw the other night, they had their work cut out.

I can't belieeeeve it's the same guy. The universe had a sick sense of humor. For example, right now, she had this strange urge to do another take. But this time she wouldn't zip him up.

What? No. He's such a pig.

She turned her head and took in the room. "This place is a mess. What happened?" Empty liquor bottles and candy bar wrappers cluttered the table near the window, the bedding was on the floor, and a collection of swords and knives were piled up on the dresser right below the wall-mounted flat screen.

"I am a lethal ex-assassin, not a maid. And I do not wish any mort—I mean strangers in my room, for obvious reasons."

Sadie sighed. She couldn't work in here like this. And she certainly wasn't going to clean up after the guy. The other option, her apartment, was way too small for someone this big to move around or do any of the exercises.

"We'll work at the beach." She'd just gone the other day with a few friends from her acting group, so she still had her picnic blanket, umbrella, and beach chair in the trunk of her car.

He gave her a look. "I did not bring suitable attire for the beach. We shall work here." He glanced at the bed.

She didn't know if he'd meant anything by that little look, but she needed to nip it in the bud. Not that the guy's body wasn't smokin' hot and his face—short black beard, simmering turquoise eyes, plump bad-boy lips meant for melting a girl's heart as he asked forgiveness for whatever stupid thing he'd just done—wasn't gorgeous, but he was rude, crude, and barbaric.

Then why does your hand feel like it's on fire from grabbing his dick through his leather pants.

"It's too stuffy in here," she said. "And for the record, before you get any ideas, I'm into gentlemen, which we both know you're not."

"And for the record, I am *not* into little girls, which we both know you are." He dipped his head.

Okay, you. That was mean.

But I did insult his manhood. Maybe I deserved it?

On the other hand, he called me plain. And he got me fired.

Stop, Sadie. Get to work. Think: one hundred thousand dollars. That's life-changing money.

She took a deep breath and then pulled herself back together. "Can I be honest with you? I really need this job, and from what I've heard, you really want this part you're up for. And I know we don't know each other, but it seems like we might need one another. So how about we put down our swords and help each other?"

He didn't reply. Instead, he stood glaring at her with his hard eyes as if trying to figure something out.

She continued, "I really think we should be somewhere with plenty of room to move around. I'll try to find a new place for us tomorrow, but let's try the beach today. It's beautiful and sunny outside, just perfect for a little acting inspiration. Okay?"

He narrowed his beautiful eyes in contemplation. "You are a very strange, yet oddly persuasive woman."

"I'll take that as a compliment," she said, inspecting his insanely fit body. Damn, he was huge. They probably wouldn't have anything beach-like that would fit him down in the lobby. "Would you happen to have any jeans?"

He jerked his head toward a black duffle bag thrown in the corner. "In there," he said. "Why? Are you planning to strangle me with them?"

She walked over, unzipped the bag, and pulled it open. Right at the top was an unframed photo of a little girl. Blonde curls, big blue eyes, with her arms thrown around Andrus's neck and kissing his cheek. He looked like a completely different person—glowing, happy, smiling.

"Oh, I didn't realize you have kids," she said. "And why are you holding a sword in the air?"

He walked over and snatched the photo from her hand. "I don't have children, and none of your business."

Okay. She saw the wad of faded denim and pulled them from the bag. "These will work."

"For what?" he asked.

She grabbed one of the sharp-looking knives on the dresser and made a little slice above the knee.

"Hold on, woman. Those are my favorite jeans," he protested while she ripped.

"Now they're your favorite shorts. And call me 'woman' one more time, I will cut off your man berries." She made another slit and tore the other leg. "Here. Put these on."

He stared at her, his gaze somewhere between irritated and deadly. He was a very convincing actor.

Slowly, he shed his leather pants, dropping them to the floor. His thick cock hung low between his powerful thighs, which were dusted with dark hair.

She gulped, unable to take her eyes away from his substantial penis.

"Drink it in, meat wench. This teeny weeny is the closest you'll ever get to such perfection," he said, his deep, baritone voice filled with arrogance.

Her eyes snapped up to meet his devilish gaze. "Oh, get over yourself. I'll wait outside."

She left the room and slammed the door shut behind her, feeling like she couldn't breathe. The man was...was...he was a cocky tyrant.

And what just happened in there? He'd made her so scatterbrained that she'd acted like some insane woman. But something about him felt so different. Almost like she fed off of his crazy energy. It made her all giddy and smart-mouthed and fearless.

Oh my God. Did I really grab that man's crotch? She started to laugh. *Wow, I really got into character.* But if she didn't somehow manage to get focused around him, he wouldn't be ready for his part, she wouldn't get paid, and she'd lose everything.

Okay, Sadie. You can do this. You can do this. You are strong, independent and a fighter. She would not allow this man's raw masculinity and overbearing machismo to get in the way of getting the job done.

An image of him standing bottomless flashed in her mind. She'd never seen a more well-endowed, gorgeous, manly brick of muscles.

This was going to be one hell of a week.

After Sadie left his room, Andrus stood staring at the door, feeling winded and speechless. That woman was abrasive, bossy, and so godsdamned cruel, using her sexy little moves and body as a weapon against him. And the way she grabbed his cock, fearless and brazen, made him feel dizzy with lust.

Who did she think she was, trying to subdue him with her feminine wiles? Did she think he was born yesterday?

If she weren't so beautiful, he would've taken her over his knee and taught her a lesson. *Oh, wait. That sounds really nice.* The thought of a little rough play with this saucy she-devil struck a sinful chord. She definitely brought out the dirty boy in him.

Oddly enough, he'd actually been thinking of her when he tried to pop off a round just now. There'd been a moment at the restaurant, lying over her body, his cock snugly wedged between her thighs, that he couldn't get out of his mind. She'd felt damned fantastic.

Wait. This smells...fishy.

He shook his head from side to side. It was no coincidence that his "teacher" was the sexy woman from the restaurant.

Yes, this smells suspicious. Cimil is up to something. The issue being, one never knew what she was up to because her brain functioned in such a twisted manner that it was impossible to predict the angles. But one thing he knew for certain was that crazy goddess would always pretend to help while she led you into shark-infested waters. If you were lucky enough to survive, you'd surely be a few limbs short. She was the master of sadistic mind games, mayhem, and driving people to the brink of insanity, simply for the pleasure of watching them suffer.

He rubbed his whisker-covered jaw. So what was Cimil up to? If she said that his second-chance mate was going to be at the party in six days, it was likely a lie. He'd show up to the party and find himself playing a pawn in some other game.

No. That sounds too straightforward.

Perhaps Cimil wished to dangle Sadie, who clearly disapproved of him, in his face just to make him squirm? Well, this Sadie certainly was sexy, but he squirmed for no woman. Of course, Cimil would know that.

It makes no sense. What is that evil goddess up to?

The little meat wench pounded on the door. "Hurry up in there!"

He stared at the door. *Hmmm...* So Cimil wanted this sexy little vixen to teach him to "act" like a gentlemen so he could impress this Charlotte woman. However, everyone knew that mates were drawn to one another, so he'd bet that Cimil's little speech about wooing had been a lie. Besides, even if he managed to woo the woman for a few minutes by behaving like some pompous, smooth-tongued Dapper Dan, what purpose would that serve? He was who he was—deadly, fierce, loyal, and...did he mention deadly? He was unapologetically male and damned proud of it. So this Charlotte, whoever she was, would have to love him for his true self: a three-hundred-year-old—give or take a few decades—immortal assassin. *An ancient lethal warrior.*

That settles it. I'm not going to play along.

He then thought about Matty. If Cimil wasn't lying, then he could derail her little life.

Andrus blew out a breath.

"Hey! Are you touching yourself again?" Sadie pounded on the door. "What are you? Sixteen? Do that on your own sweet time!"

Andrus had an idea. Cimil had obviously promised Sadie something in return for playing a part in the little plan. She had to be in on it. *I'll seduce the truth out of this little minx and turn her to Team Andrus.*

He slid on his cutoffs, grabbed his leather, steel-toed boots, and took a look in the mirror. He smiled and then pivoted to look at his ass. "Hmmm...not bad."

CHAPTER SEVEN

Sadie had argued in the hotel parking lot with the big man for ten entire minutes before she finally gave in. They would take his outrageously earth-unfriendly gas-guzzler to the beach instead of her fuel-efficient, emerald-green, hybrid Kia Soul.

She sat in the passenger seat as he loaded her beach gear into the back of his black SUV. "This is completely ridiculous. You will fit in my car. You're not a hippopotamus!"

He hopped into the driver's side and shut his door, gloating like a smug jackass. "Sorry. However, cocks like mine need a little breathing room."

She rolled her eyes. "You're so full of yourself. I'm surprised you don't tow around a trailer on the back of this thing just to carry around your ego."

He cranked the engine and snickered. "Or to carry around my enormous cock."

Oh my God. This guy... "It's a good thing you're not lacking in the self-love department, because I can't imagine anyone being able to put up with you."

He turned his body, about to back out, but stopped and looked at her with smoldering eyes. "I promise not to judge you when you finally admit to wanting me, my fierce little rabbit."

Fierce little rabbit? "My name is Sadie. Sadie Townsend. And I promise not to laugh at you when you start crying because it finally sinks in I will never want you."

At least for more than just a few little glances at your body and the occasional sex dream, which absolutely doesn't count because I have no control over those.

"Sadie," he purred her name in a deep, velvety, bedroom voice. "It means princess." He reached over and traced his finger along her collarbone. "But I think I shall call you Sexy Sadie, like the song."

For a brief moment, her body trembled from the sensual sensation of him touching her skin. *Wait. Why's he hitting on me?* Did he sense her lack of interest and now felt it necessary to prove to himself that he could get her into bed?

Why do I always attract the aggressive lunatics? For example, the last guy she went out with, before Tim, turned out to be a stalker. No. A real one. After just one date, he started showing up at her apartment late at night, to her work, and followed her to the grocery store. When she realized that telling him to go away wasn't going to do the trick, she filed a restraining order. Thankfully, he stopped coming around right about the time she met Tim. Then there was her last boyfriend back home, whom she'd dated for six months. Unbeknownst to her, he liked to come to her window at night and watch her sleep. She finally found out when her father caught him. Anyway, they weren't all complete weirdos, but she definitely reeled in men from the oddball end of the spectrum.

"I think you should call me coach," she said. "And if you must, Coach Sadie." There. That would establish a professional boundary.

"Coach Sexy Sadie. I like it." He backed out, nearly running over a Fiat in the process. "Ah. There, you see? Had we been in your little woman-wagon, you would be dead. I have saved you."

Sadie clenched her eyes shut. *Dear Lord, please give me the strength to not strangle the barbarian.* "I am praying that was your character talking, because if you're really this big of a man-pig, there are no amount of acting lessons that can help you."

"I assure you I am every bit the man-pig you just accused me of being, and I offer no apologies. If it weren't for men such as myself, you'd all be sex slaves to packs of psychopathic, blood-drinking rapists."

Her head whipped in his direction. "Jesus. Dark much, Andrus?"

"You have no fucking idea."

Sadie was about to speak when she noticed he suddenly radiated that same lethal vibe she'd seen at the restaurant. Only this time, it didn't make her nervous as much as it intrigued her. His technique for taking on personas and creating a mood was phenomenal.

"I know I'm going to kick myself for saying this, Andrus. But you really are pretty impressive."

He smiled and flashed her a cocky grin. "So I've been told."

She huffed out a breath and rolled her eyes. "Knew I'd regret that." More importantly, she was beginning to wonder something. This man might not be a dignitary or the embodiment of civilized gentlemen, but he seemed like a very capable actor. She hadn't seen one lapse in this persona he'd taken on.

Something about this situation felt...off.

Welp. No choice now but to move forward. She just hoped he got the role.

⁂

After an awkwardly quiet drive, they'd parked and found a somewhat quieter spot under a palm tree on the crowded beach. It was Sunday, so the crowds were typical for a sunny fall weekend, but the beach still had way more room to walk around and practice some role-playing.

"So, Andrus," she said, laying out her red beach blanket. "I assume you're doing some kind of action film. What's the setting? Air carrier, skyscraper, urban sprawl?"

A woman in a very tiny pink bikini strolled by, and Andrus just stared.

Okay, maybe the beach was a bad idea.

"Did you see that one?" he asked. "Her ass is hanging out. Her parents should be informed." His head flipped in the other direction as a blonde in a black thong bikini jogged by. "Good gods. Were they raised in a brothel?"

"Don't you think you're being a little harsh?" she said. "Especially coming from someone who showed me his penis about an hour ago?"

"That was very different," he said, in a deep authoritative voice. "I am a man and you are a grown woman. Those females are children, no older than seventeen or eighteen."

"I thought you said I was a little girl." She flipped out her blue folding chair.

"I was referring to your mental age; however, if you wore something so revealing to a public beach and you were my woman, I would throw you over my shoulder and give your exposed ass cheeks a lesson with my hand."

The mental image of that was wrong in so, so many ways, yet it somehow turned her the hell on.

No. No, it didn't. You definitely do not want to be flung over his shoulder and spanked. And it was a chauvinistic thing to say. Of course, he is just acting. At least...I hope he is.

"Andrus, what time period is your character from?"

He stared blankly.

"Oh sorry." He was in character. "What year were you born?"

"1683."

Well, the time period explained the deep-rooted chauvinism. "So you're doing a historical action film?"

He grinned. "It's more of a romance."

"Oh, boy. Then we really have our work cut out. So our first lesson is going to be about how to speak to a woman—"

He stood up. "I think I'll go for a swim. Care to join me?"

"What?"

"A swim. It's been centuries since I've been in the ocean."

"Centuries, huh? Well, I'm sorry, but no. We need to work, Andrus. I have less than a week to get you ready, or I don't get paid."

"You should've negotiated for a better deal." He kicked off his boots and stripped off his shirt.

Holy mother of God.

As her eyes scaled up his abs, the deep grooves of his washboard stomach flexing with fiercely seductive power, she found herself mesmerized. The light olive skin of his bare arms and chest and...*Oh my God. This guy is built like an evil sexy tank.* And whether she liked it or not, her female libido reacted—nipple tingles, core flutters, the whole nine yards. *Or ten inches, in his case.*

Andrus caught her blatantly drooling and then winked. "You're welcome." He dipped his head of thick, messy dark hair, turned, and slowly made his way toward the water.

Sadie watched along with every other woman within eyeshot. They all stopped whatever they were doing—volleyball, applying suntan oil, kissing their boyfriends, or avoiding trees while they were rollerblading—*Watch out! Oh, that had to hurt.* Even the men stopped to fume in Andrus's general direction, seething with a territorial-type jealousy as he practically floated over the sand, his naturally tanned muscles flexing and pumping in a hypnotic rhythm as he strolled toward the waves.

He looked like a fucking god. Tall, lean, menacing ropes of—

He jumped head first into a wave, startling Sadie from her little sexually charged, mental detour.

"Wow." Okay. She had to admit, there was something about the man that was different. Almost like he was from another world, shamelessly defying all the rules. She, for example, found his attitude repugnant and chauvinistic, yet he'd still managed to get her to gawk. And that body? Sinfully sexy in a way that spoke to some hidden quiet female animal inside her.

Sadie sat staring at the waves, trying to figure out what exactly it was about the man that made him so annoyingly seductive, when she realized he hadn't come up for air.

The surf didn't look all that rough today, but the flags on the lifeguard towers were yellow. Some undertow.

Before permitting herself to panic, she stood and began scanning the waves and bobbing heads out beyond the break. Only a few surfers and boogie boarders paddled around. *No Andrus.*

Okay. Now I'm worried. She started jogging toward the spot where he dove in, looking for any sign of the big man.

Nothing.

Oh, hell. Just my luck. The man can't swim.

She turned toward the lifeguard shack, but the tower was empty. *Oh my God. Oh my God.*

She looked back toward the waves, completely freaking the hell out. Just then, a large wave crested and came crashing in. She caught a glimpse of a body rolling in the white water.

"Andrus! Shit!" She charged into the waves, fighting the current to get to him, but when she got to the spot, he wasn't there. *No, no, no. Where is he?* A wave slammed into her body, knocking her over. She fought to get her head back up, twisting every which way in the water, searching for him.

Then her eyes spotted his limp form lying facedown in the shallow waves.

"Fuck!" She used her arms to jog through the water, making her way to him. "Andrus. Andrus!"

By then a few others had noticed him lying there and were rushing over.

She dropped to her knees, panting hard, and flipped him over. His beautiful face was covered in wet sand, but he didn't look blue.

"No, dammit." He wasn't breathing.

She jumped on top of him and started compressions. Luckily, CPR was a class she'd had in high school—her mother's insistence when she began babysitting her younger sister.

Sadie popped open his mouth and tilted back his head to position the tongue and gave him a puff. Then another.

She suddenly felt a soft, warm tongue slide inside her mouth, flicking against her own tongue.

What the fuc—

Two strong arms wrapped around her, simultaneously flipping her back to the sand. He kissed her hard, pinning her with half his body, holding her tight with those big bulky biceps.

Sonofabitch. She bit down on his lip, and he pulled away.

"Ow. That hurt," he whined.

"You dirty, horrible sonofabitch!" She pounded his shoulder with her fist. "I thought you were dead."

He grinned devilishly. "Oops. I guess not. But I'm flattered to find that you care so much." His lips shot toward her mouth, and she turned her head, trying to wiggle away.

"Get the hell off me!"

He let her go and began laughing with a deep, hearty chuckle. "What? I just wanted a kiss."

She popped to her feet. "Nothing to see, everyone," she said to the crowd who'd gathered around—all women, of course. "The asshole was just faking it." She marched off to go get her stuff. This was ridiculous.

"Wait. Sadie," Andrus said, catching up to her, "I was merely having a little fun. Come on…"

He made an attempt to grab her arm, and she jerked it away. "Fuck the hell off, you sick bastard."

"Oh. Come now. You know you liked it."

What a complete and total pig! She swiveled on her heel. "Is this some joke to you? Is it? Because it's not to me. I need this job. I need this money. Don't you get that? Don't you have any idea how hard I work just to have a chance to live my dream?"

No longer smiling, he looked down at her with those thick lashes and turquoise eyes. "Fantastic acting, my little meat wench, but I'm not buying it."

"Buying what?" she fumed.

"We both know you're not here to help me. But if you come clean and tell me everything, I'll let you have a night in my bed."

"Oh my god," she snarled. "You really are a prick. And you sure as hell don't deserve the chance you're being given. Anyone I know would kill to have the opportunity for a movie role. Hell, I would kill for it. But here you are, pissing it away, which makes you an even bigger ass than I thought."

She marched off, feeling like she actually might kill the man. Kill him. With a butter knife.

"Keep up the acting, woman! You are quite marvelous at it," she heard him call out from a distance.

CHAPTER EIGHT

Mother of all things tempting and delicious. Zac stared at Tula's creamy smooth calves as she bent over, watering the new plants she'd had delivered this morning. *She'll be the death of me.*

Over the last several days, she'd worn a knee-length skirt with daisies, an ankle-length dress with blue squiggly things, and some other outfit that had a high neckline. None of her outfits were tight or sexy or revealing. In fact, they covered too much. But that was what made it so hard to look away. The more prim and proper she dressed, the bigger the prize of tempting her.

"Dammit, Tula. Can't you wear something slutty to work for once? Something that might shame your family or get you mistakenly arrested for prostitution? I can't get any damned work done around here!"

She tilted up her watering can and slowly turned. "You feelin' okay, Mr. Zac?"

"No," he grumbled and shifted his eyes back down to his laptop screen.

"It's the decorations, isn't it? They're irritating you," she said, sounding disappointed.

Hell no. She'd done a great job. She'd brought in

another desk and a black leather chair—a badass chair—just for him and made a little waiting area near the elevator, complete with a huge flat screen, two colorful red sofas, and some end tables. She'd even had the landlord bring in these very ingenious moveable walls to make a kitchen area with a coffee machine, fridge, and table for sitting and eating lunch. Which she did every day, innocently nibbling on whatever wholesome food she prepared while she perused wedding magazines.

The place still had a ton of empty space, but at least it felt homier, and he could catch his favorite show, *American Ninja*.

I love watching humans try to be like us gods. Very amusing. What wasn't amusing was her nunlike disposition and infallible moral fiber. *Gods, I just want to tie her up and lick her from head to toe until she gives in to me.*

"The furnishings are fine, Tula. I simply find it difficult to concentrate when you behave so anti-seductively or wear such unsexy clothing."

"You're weird, Mr. Zac." She turned and went back to watering the plants near the window in her most non-sexy way.

He groaned, adjusted his cock, and went back to his task of screening invitees for the mixer. So far, he'd approved everyone with the exception of a fucking Maaskab—holy fucking gods, was that some sort of joke? He'd have to ask Cimil later—

and his brother Acan, the God of Wine and Intoxication, better known as Belch. It was a waste to have Belch attend as a guest because A) who in their right mind would want to date that drunk slob? And B) he was the best bartender on the planet. He could look right at a person and know exactly what drink to serve, even when they didn't know themselves. He also accidentally lit a lot of shit on fire, which always made for a more interesting party. *Belch is definitely tending bar.*

Zac scribbled on his notepad: *Have Tula order extra fire extinguishers for mixer.*

The elevator door chimed and out stepped a gorgeous woman with soft waves of auburn hair and golden-brown eyes, wearing sweet little tiny shorts and a tight tank top showing off her plump breasts and curvy hips.

"Well, well, how may I help you today, Miss?" he said in his best and most tempting voice.

She looked around at the empty office. "Where the hell is Bob?"

"Bob? I'm not sure you—"

Cimil's office door swung open. "Sippy, baby. Nice to see you!"

What the fuck?

Cimil wore a short brown wig, mustache, and gray plaid suit.

"Uh, Cimil," Zac said, "why are you dressed as—"

"Shut it, Zac, or I will instruct Tula to sing church

hymns every day, all day, for the next year."

Zac snapped his mouth shut. He also wondered just exactly when Cimil had shown up. He hadn't seen her go into the office. *So fucking weird.*

"Sadie," Cimil said in a deep, worst man-voice ever, "won't you come into my office?"

Sadie or Sippy—whatever—marched right in and slammed the door shut. But with his super-deific hearing, he could make out almost every word:

Andrus.

Asshole.

Want him dead now.

How could you do this to me?

Bastard.

Showed his cock.

Faked drowning.

Kissed me.

Propositioned me.

Twice.

Threatened me with large knife.

Got me fired.

Hate you, Bob.

Wow. Zac laughed. *I need to hang out with Andrus more often.*

Then Cimil, in her man-voice, tried to assure the mortal that everything would be handled.

"You'd better, Bob," the woman screeched. "Because if I don't get paid, then neither do you."

The door flew open and the woman stormed out

toward the stairs, not bothering to wait for the elevator.

"Zac!" Cimil barked. "Get in here."

Oh, with pleasure. And a side of rubbing it in coming right up, too! Zac entered the office and Cimil looked genuinely bothered. That did not sit well with him. Why? Because nothing ever bothered Cimil.

"Shut the door," she said, sitting on her desk, ripping off her fake mustache. "This isn't working."

"What's not working?"

"This!" She threw up her pale boney hands. "I can't do it. I can't shoot straight."

"Mind elaborating, oh crazy one?"

"Everything is going wrong. And do you know why?"

"Because you're predisposed to destroying all life on the planet while simultaneously saving everyone?" he guessed.

"No!" Her finger shot up. "For the first time in my existence, I am being honest."

Yeah, right. Don't believe that for a minute, but I'll play along. "And?"

"It's ruining everything! Andrus is supposed to fall in love with Charlotte, his second-chance mate, in five days. That woman Sadie—" she pointed to the door "—is supposed to show him how to be a better wooer. But now he refuses to be instructed by her because he thinks I'm deceiving him, up to my old tricks when clearly I'm not."

"Oh. Now I see."

"You have to talk to him, Zac. Asshole to asshole. Immortal male pig to immortal male pig. Convince him that he must listen to the actress. Convince him this is his only chance."

"I'm not sure I'm convinced you're telling the truth either, Cimil."

She rolled her eyes. "Have I been nothing but honest since we came here?"

He shrugged and glanced toward the door, but his eyes were envisioning Tula's sweet little ankles.

"Zac, she is not for you. She is the Fort Knox of vaginas. You can't break her. You can't seduce her. She loves another and always will."

"Soooo, you're trying to tell me that she's not some attempt to make me suffer needlessly and then, after months, perhaps years of suffering, she'll leave her fiancé and realize she wants to bed me?"

Cimil shook her head. "Nope. Never gonna happen."

He tilted his head.

"I'm serious!" Cimil screamed, throwing her arms down at her sides. "And if you don't believe me, go out there right now and lay it on her. Give it all you got."

"Seriously?" Zac asked.

"Yeah." Cimil gestured toward the door. "Be my guest."

If Cimil was telling the truth about Tula, there

was one sure way to find out.

He marched out of Cimil's office. "Tula!"

Tula looked up from her desk nervously. "What's the matter?"

"Come here." He plucked her from her chair, grabbed her by the waist, pulled her in tight, and kissed her with every trick in the temptation toolbox: soft sensual lips, sinful movements of his tongue, and the warm vibrations of his body. He kissed her until he felt his energy spiking to maximum levels. Mortals and deities created a reaction, the result generally being the mortal dropping dead if exposed for too long, unless the human wore black jade—a material used to blunt a deity's energy.

Before he fried her, he let go and dropped his hands. He stared down at the small, wholesome woman, waiting for her response.

She blinked her big blues at him and then smiled shyly. "Mr. Zac, while that was a lovely kiss, I'm afraid I'm set to marry Gilbert. And since he and I don't swing, it's just never gonna happen between you and me." She shrugged. "But a big delicious god like you will find your special someone. I'm sure of it." She poked his chest.

Damned woman! She hadn't even broken a sweat or moaned or...anything. Even her objection was sweet and wholesome.

He turned back toward Cimil's office and slammed the door. "Fine. I believe you. Tula is immune to my charms."

Of course, now he wanted her more than ever. *Ah! Gods fucking bloody hell! Now what am I going to do?* She was like the last piece of chocolate on earth. So tempting.

"Good," Cimil said. "Now go knock some sense into Andrus so we can move on to the next client. We have to hurry before we run out of time."

"What do you mean, 'run out'?"

"You know," she replied, "before you go all crazy and start killing everyone."

What the devil? "What are you talking about, Cimil?"

"Don't you remember? I foresee you losing your marbles and then you go on a rampage, murdering everyone. I think it's because you're here too long, but I'm not sure."

"I think," he growled, "you forgot to mention this."

She shrugged. "That's weird. I coulda sworn I told you."

"When does this happen?"

"I dunno. I keep hearing the dead scream your name, but without my powers, I can't get a good read on what happens."

He dropped his head. "Bloody fuck. Just great. We need to call for a meeting of the gods before that happens."

"Sorry." Cimil shook her head. "I already tried. They think it's just another one of my secret evil plots."

Perhaps it was. No one ever knew for certain. On the other hand, if she was telling the truth, which happened about fifty percent of the time, then they really needed to fucking hurry the hell up. *I refuse to become the God of Mass Murder.* That did not have a cool ring to it at all.

"I'll call Andrus and get him on board," he grumbled miserably.

"Great! If he refuses to listen, call Helena. If anyone can get him to see reason, it's her."

"Fine. Got it," he replied. "And Cimil? When this is all over, I'm going to make you pay."

"Oh, goody!" She clapped. "Do you take fives and singles? I've foreseen I will take up stripping."

CHAPTER NINE

After the beach incident with Sadie, Andrus decided the best course of action was to leave town. For some reason, her final comments had gotten under his skin, even though he knew she had been referring to him pissing away a chance at some nonexistent acting job.

Still, her comments hit a nerve, and he wasn't sure why. Perhaps because he wanted the opportunity she hadn't spoken of—a true chance of finding someone to share eternity with. But in his heart, he simply couldn't believe it would be given to him. After enduring centuries of heartache with his last mate and then losing Matty and Helena from his life, he didn't have the courage to venture down yet another path that would lead to disappointment. It simply felt easier to be alone.

Hope is for suckers.

So he'd packed up his shit, checked out of the hotel, and got into his rental Hummer. Sadie's car was gone from the parking lot, so he knew she'd already come to retrieve it.

That woman was quite the little actress, pretending innocently to be helping him while they both knew she worked for Cimil.

Oddly, it kind of bothered him, which irritated

him more because he didn't know the woman.

However, now more than ever, he felt convinced this was all some plan to simply amuse the Goddess of the Underworld. He now saw how Cimil had used his emotions against him, leveraging little Matty to get him to do whatever she wanted. But logic said there were no second mates. There was one and only one. That didn't mean he wouldn't someday meet a woman whose company he enjoyed; it simply meant that the fire might not be everlasting and that their connection would be less consuming. Hell, what was wrong with that?

He'd been mated before, and it fucking sucked. The woman had complete control over him, could get him to do anything just to be near her.

He much preferred a normal relationship. Possibly none at all. *Yes, one-nighters are perfect.* And a man like him could have an endless supply.

Miami, here I come, he thought, pulling onto the freeway and immediately hitting the brakes. *Fucking L.A.* How did people actually travel anywhere when rush hour started at 6:00 a.m. and ended at 10:00 p.m. seven days a week?

His cell phone rang, and he hit the Bluetooth on the steering wheel. "Yeah?"

"Hello, Andrus, it's I, Zac, God of Temptation."

Oh, marvelous. Cimil's sidekick. "Aren't you the ex-God of Temptation since you're now powerless?"

"I'll get my powers back. Someday. It might

happen a little fucking faster if you'd play ball."

"Forget it. I'm not getting sucked into whatever scheme Cimil's got going."

"Andrus, I'm going to lay it on you, one badass immortal to another: Cimil isn't fucking around. At least, I don't think she is."

This coming from a god who believed Cimil when she told him he could steal away his brother's mate by using his powers. Two huge no-nos according to their sacred laws. "Sorry. I'm heading to the airport."

"Fine," Zac sighed on the phone, "I didn't want to do this, but you give me no choice."

Oh, this ought to be good. Andrus chuckled and looked at himself in the rearview mirror, inspecting his pearly whites. Traffic hadn't moved one inch, so he could do with a little amusement.

"Andrus?" said a soft female voice. "It's Helena."

Andrus felt his blood chill. Hearing the sound of her voice felt like a stab to the heart.

He swallowed back his emotions. "Helena, so they've dragged you into this, have they? What did Cimil promise you? A ride on her unicorn?"

"Andrus," Helena said, "I know that you're probably furious with me given the way I kicked you out. And I know you don't owe me any favors, but I'm begging. Please do what Cimil is asking."

Andrus laughed. "This? Coming from you?" Cimil had put Niccolo, her mate, to sleep for three hundred years to await Helena's birth. Then she told him he couldn't touch her—a complete lie—for three months. It nearly drove them both mad. There was a lot more to the story, but the moral was, never trust Cimil. Not ever.

"I know what you're thinking," Helena said, "but despite her unethical, sadistic, and crazy ways, everything always works out in the end. She just enjoys making it painful."

"No. Sometimes things don't work out. Need I remind you of the clowns?" he asked.

"Okay. Except for the clowns. Although, no one knows what Cimil did with them, so there's still a chance it could work out."

Not likely. Cimil had it in for the clowns and had rounded up hundreds, perhaps thousands, of them. No one had seen or heard from them since.

She continued, "The point is, most of the time, Cimil isn't lying. If she says you're supposed to meet this woman and be the father of Matty's mate, then why risk it? The party is only a few days away."

"Five days. And no. I'm not going. I care deeply for Matty, but I do not wish to meet this woman, even if she is my mate."

"But, Andrus—"

"I have no interest, Helena, in being tethered to another woman. May I remind you how well that worked out for me the last time?"

Helena knew every detail. She'd been there during those final moments when his mate tried to kill him. Ironically, Niccolo showed up and stabbed her.

Helena started to cry. "But what will Matty do for the rest of her life, Andrus? Be alone and bitter like..." her voice trailed off.

"Like me. You were about to say 'like me,' weren't you?"

"She deserves a chance at happiness."

"But I don't. I don't deserve that, now do I?" Helena knew he loved her. It was the reason he'd stayed to protect her even after she'd married Niccolo.

"I'm sorry, Andrus. I'm sorry you're not the one. But you are family and I do love you, just not the way you need me to."

"Like a brother," he said bitterly.

"No. Like my daughter's father-in-law."

Ouch. That was far worse. "So that is all I am to you? Merely the sperm donor to create your daughter's future husband?"

"Yes. Okay, you're my friend, too, but mostly I just love you for your sperm."

Andrus heard Niccolo belting out Italian cuss words in the background.

"Oh, be quiet!" she yelled back. "Can't I talk about another man's sperm without you getting your leather pants in a tizzy? You're such an ogre!" She returned to the conversation. "Please, Andrus. Five more days. Meet the woman. Give her your sperm. And then you can go wherever you like.

Except New York City. Don't come here. I think Niccolo might castrate you, and I'm sure you love your testicles."

Andrus heard more yelling in the background.

"No!" she yelled. "I did not say I love his testicles—would you stop listening in? Go do some laundry or warm up some blood for my lunch." She returned to the conversation. "Sorry. I swear, that man is over a thousand years old, but still acts like he's five."

If only I had a mate, that could be my life. I dare to dream.

"I have to go, Andrus, but Matty and I will come see you soon. She misses you."

"I must go now."

"Please promise you'll at least think about it?" she asked.

"I will reconsider."

"Good. Because the Andrus I know never ran away from anything. Not even Cimil."

Grrrrr. She knew that would push his damned buttons.

"Hey, man." Zac's voice came through the speaker. He'd been on the line listening in the entire time. "I'll text you Sadie's address. Cimil recommends you keep it in your pants from now on."

"I didn't agree to—"

"Hey, you're preaching to the choir, Andrus. I think staying single for eternity is the way to go. I mean, there are only so many immortals out there and millions of humans to play with. I bet that little Matty won't mind spreading the love around once she's all grown up and mateless."

Andrus instantly felt enraged. The thought of men, lots of them, laying their hands on her made him furious. "You're an asshole, Zac."

"Did it work?"

"Yes. Text the address, please." The moment he said those words, he experienced an odd little glow in his heart. And perhaps a bit lower, too. He actually felt excited to see Sadie again?

Crap. I must be losing my mind. But that kiss, he now realized, had been replaying in the back of his mind. It had felt oddly arousing. *No, it's simply been too long since you've bedded a woman. This is all.*

Yes, that had to be it. However, just to be sure, perhaps he should kiss her again?

No, you idiot. You should not. You are to meet this...mate woman.

Two hours later—*Damned L.A. traffic!*—Andrus pulled up to a dingy, pea-green apartment complex in Hollywood. For clarification purposes, it was not a nice neighborhood. One could practically smell the malevolence and human decay in the air.

Parked on the street out front, he grabbed his sword, strapped it to his back, and threw on his leather duster. Unfortunately, it was hotter than hell today, but cooking was far better than being unprepared.

He exited the vehicle and made the usual sweep of the surrounding area with his eyes. Late model cars lined the street, and the neighborhood was densely packed with run-down apartment buildings and an Indian restaurant. Garbage littered the sidewalks, and some unruly sorts hung out on the corner in front of a liquor store. They were trying to be casual about it, but the men seemed very interested in his vehicle.

Andrus shot them all a look, using his eyes to send a clear message. *Touch the car, you die.* The men scattered with the stench-filled wind.

This is where she lives? It was no place for a single woman, let alone anyone unarmed. *Or not of the rat species.*

He made his way to the side of the building, stepping over a man who'd decided to take a nap with his empty gin bottle in the middle of the stairs. Suddenly, he scented something unusual in the air, and it wasn't the drunk's urine-stained pants or the burning curry coming from the restaurant next door.

When he found apartment 2E toward the end of the hall, the strange scent became stronger.

"Sadie?" He knocked on the pea-green, graffiti-covered door. Several long moments passed, but she didn't answer. "Sadie, it's Andrus." *Obviously, you idiot. Not like the woman forgot your manly voice in the space of a few hours.*

He gave the door one more knock, debating if he should come again later; however, something—that strange scent perhaps—made him feel uneasy. He tried the door and found it unlocked.

He pushed it open, gripping the handle of his sword behind his neck. Sadie sat in the middle of the cramped, dingy room on her small bed, staring at the wall.

"Sadie?"

She did not respond, but that strange smell permeated the room.

His eyes made a quick sweep of the tiny space. A small bathroom in the corner. A closet. Aside from that, there wasn't much else apart from a kitchenette and bed. *No room for anything more.*

Cautiously, he walked to the closet, listening for signs of an intruder. He slowly drew his sword, not making a sound, not breathing. He pushed open the closet door—one of those accordion types—ready to strike, but found it empty of any persons.

He then checked the bathroom and underneath the bed. All the while, Sadie remained in a daze, staring at the wall.

He put away his sword and then turned his attention to her. She wore black shorts and a white tank top and had scratches up and down her legs as well as welts on her pale arms. Her hair was messed up, as if she'd had a ponytail but had been in a struggle, some of the locks falling loose around her shoulders.

"Sadie?" he said quietly, careful not to startle her. He'd seen the same look in his men's eyes after a bloody battle. Standing over her, he reached out and gently touched her shoulder. "Can you hear me?"

The moment he made contact with her skin, she jumped from the bed and screamed. "What the fuck?" She pressed her back to the wall, holding out her hands defensively. It took a moment for her to register who he was. "What the hell are you doing here?"

"I came to talk to you."

"Did ya think to knock? I mean, who just comes in and wakes a person when they're taking a nap?"

He studied her for a moment. "Do you normally nap sitting upright while staring at the wall?"

She gave him a look. "What the hell are you talking about?"

"What happened to your legs, Sadie?" Her eyes followed his gaze down to her thighs.

"Oh my God," she gasped her words. "What did you do to me?"

"Me? I found you like this." Something strange was definitely happening. "Do you recall anyone here with you?"

She shook her head. "No. I mean, Tim came by earlier, but he left and then I lay down for a nap."

"Who is Tim?"

"My boyfriend—well, he was, but I broke up with him. At least, I think I did. I don't remember."

That didn't sound right. "Where does this Tim live?"

She scratched the back of her head. "I don't know, actually. I remember going to his place, but can't remember where it is. Why? What do you want with him?"

Someone had done something bad to her and then made her forget. His first thought was this reeked of Obscuro—an evil vampire—but they'd all been wiped out. Not that more couldn't be created, but the smell in the air was unlike anything he'd ever come across.

Definitely not vampire.

"Do you know anyplace else I might be able to find him?" Andrus asked.

"Ummm...he owns an art gallery, but I can't remember where that is either."

Shit. She'd definitely had her memory toyed with.

"But I do remember giant vaginas," she offered.

He gave her a look. "Giant vaginas?"

"Yeah, it was an exhibit he had—walking vaginas, talking vaginas, vagina furniture."

Sounds like my kind of art. "Then it won't be too hard to track him down, I'm sure."

"Why do you want to find him?" she asked, still sounding mildly disoriented.

Andrus wasn't sure how to ask this question, but he needed to know what he was dealing with. "Sadie, someone has harmed you—there are welts on your arms and scratches on your legs. The rest of your body must be inspected."

"What?" She rolled her eyes. "Nice try, asshole."

"This is not a sexual thing. But I must know if…"

The gist, at least part of it, finally hit her. "Andrus, you're starting to frighten me."

It seemed that whatever daze she'd been in had suddenly worn off.

"I do not mean to," he said, "but…can you please go into the bathroom and remove your clothes? Tell me if you see any bite marks on your body or if you've been…you know."

"You think I've been…" She covered her mouth in horror and ran into her bathroom, slamming the door shut behind her.

Moments later she emerged in her black underwear and bra. "Okay," she said, panting, "I haven't been touched from what I can tell."

Andrus looked at her body and felt a painful shock wave of lust bolt through him. Not the time, my friend. Still, she was beautiful and it was an image he wouldn't soon forget.

Sadie must've notice him trying desperately to be a gentleman and not to look. "Oops. I forgot my clothes. I'll be right back." When she turned around, he noticed more claw marks on her back and a bite mark on the back of her shoulder. His pulse switched gears to rage mode.

"Sadie, it is not safe for you here. Please pack your belongings. Immediately. Do not plan to return."

"Andrus, I'm not leaving, but I am going to the police. I think that sleazy bastard roofied me."

"The police cannot help you. But I can."

"Listen, Andrus. You're a big macho guy. I get it. But you're an actor. This asshole may not have raped me, but he did God only knows what while I was passed out. He needs to be stopped."

All right, the rules regarding telling humans about immortals were fairly clear—it was on a need-to-know basis. She definitely needed to know because something nonhuman had been making her its lunch. He only hoped she didn't think him mad when he told her the truth.

He crossed his arms over his chest. "I am not an actor, Sadie. Just like Tim is not simply your ex-boyfriend."

Sadie began gathering up her purse and car keys, completely ignoring him. "Idiot. Thinks this is a game," she mumbled.

"I do not believe this is a game. I am not an actor. I am an assassin. Well, I was, but now I'm just an immortal."

She swiveled with her keys in her hand. "Stop it, Andrus. Can't you break character for two seconds? I'm completely freaked out right now."

Fine. He would have to show her.

Staring into her eyes, he removed his leather

duster.

"What are you doing?" she asked nervously.

He removed his sword, threw it on the bed, and then ripped off his shirt over his head.

She backed away. "Andrus, don't."

"There is nothing to fear," he said, able to smell her panic. He then slipped his dagger from his boot. "Don't scream," he said.

Sadie's golden-brown eyes widened in terror as he took the knife and plunged it right into his gut.

Terror filled her eyes. "Oh my God!" she screamed.

Ow. That fucking hurts! He pulled the knife out. "I told you not to scream! Now watch." The wound closed up and only a bit of blood had trickled out.

She pointed to his stomach, a frantic expression on her face. "What the hell was that? A fucking magic trick?"

"No." He flipped the knife and held it out to her, handle first. "Take it. The knife is real."

She took it from his hand and inspected the blade. The moment she realized it was real, she dropped it to the floor. "What the hell is going on?"

"I told you; I am immortal. Technically a demigod, although most of my existence has been as a hybrid vampire demigod, called a Demilord, created to hunt and kill evil vampires. I am simply a demigod now. My vampire bloodline died."

"Demigod? Like Percy Jackson or something?"

Sadie must not be digesting this well. Calling him

Percy Jackson was like calling the Terminator an Ewok.

"No. Demigods are immortals, generally without powers, but much stronger than humans. In my case, I'm extremely strong and well trained."

She covered her mouth. "You're serious."

Most humans were aware on some level that they were in the presence of something nonhuman—call it a hunch, gut feeling, or sixth sense, but deep down they knew. It was merely a question of believing the unbelievable.

"Quite," he responded.

She stared with an expression that reminded him of someone trying to read a map. Only the map was for a different city than the one she occupied.

"I knew there was something different about you," she finally said. "But...I don't...I'm really...I'm confused."

"Well, you may complete the 'soaking it in' phase elsewhere. Something strange is going on, and you cannot stay here."

"Andrus?" she asked, blinking her worried brown eyes at him.

"Yes?"

"Are you really a demigod?"

"Yes."

"Oh my god." She blacked out, but he caught her and laid her on the bed.

"Correction, oh my demigod."

CHAPTER TEN

Andrus had no clue what he was dealing with here, but the likely suspects were the species with the ability to glamour humans, such as shifters, who were extremely rare and even rarer in the more densely populated areas; a vampire who'd decided to stop obeying the Pact (the rules that all vampires had to obey, which included the prohibition of dining on innocent humans as determined by the color of their auras); some sort of fae, however those rarely came near humans or this world (too lowly for them); or an incubus, who'd been all but wiped out by the gods long ago. But frankly, it was the scent in Sadie's apartment that had him stumped. It was rancid and dark and unlike anything he'd ever smelled.

"So where are we going?" Sadie said, her voice void of any real emotion as they drove in his car.

"I am taking you to stay with a friend. His name is Tommaso." Andrus would send for her vehicle and come back later to collect her things. Perhaps he'd find some clue as to what attacked her.

"Is he like you?" she asked. "A—an—an immortal?"

Poor little thing. She'd awoken in his SUV, thinking it was all a dream, but when he assured her it wasn't, she simply stared at him for several long minutes. He sort of enjoyed it, actually. Then she did something unexpected: She reached out her hand and pressed it to his cheek. Considering the vehicle was in motion, he was lucky not to have crashed. Her touch, though not sexual in any way, felt oddly intimate. As if she wanted him to know she accepted him. Or was it her way of trying to accept the situation? He didn't know, but it instantly sparked something deep inside him and it took every badass bone in his badass body not to pull over and kiss her. A real kiss. Not like the one at the beach, but a kiss that allowed him to breathe her in and marinate his senses in her sweet scent— something he'd now noticed had an addictive quality.

There's simply something about her.

"Andrus?" Sadie said, prompting him to answer her question.

"Oh yes. Sorry. Tommaso is an immortal; however, he was once a Maaskab, or spy for them, really."

"Do I want to know what a Maaskab is?"

Not really. Because if you ever saw one, you would wet yourself. Unless you were with me, of course. Because I would protect you.

"They are a violent, evil sect of ancient Mayan priests who single-handedly brought down the Mayan civilization with their bloodlust and human sacrifices. They are extremely skilled at manipulating dark energy."

"Nope. I didn't want to know that," she groused.

"You have nothing to fear. Tommaso wasn't truly one of them; more like possessed by their magic and a thirst to destroy mankind. But he's all better now."

"Oh, sure. Totally nothing to worry about. So, you're going to dump me with this ex-psycho and then you're going to do what?"

"Hunt and kill Tim," he replied.

Her eyes widened. "You're going to murder someone?"

"If my suspicions are correct, he is not a someone, but a something. If I'm wrong, and he's human, then I will be sure to hand him over to Cimil, the Goddess of the Underworld."

"Cimil?"

"Cimil is Bob, your agent. Only he's a she and the Goddess of the Underworld, one of fourteen deities. She, in particular, is charged with collecting evil souls and taking them to their proper place."

"There are fourteen gods? And hell is real?" she asked, sounding like her head neared the point of exploding.

"Yes. Fourteen very disturbed, powerful, and childish gods you should steer clear of. And hell is more akin to an evil country club where their souls are contained and prevented from being recycled."

Sadie blew out a long breath. "Bob is a god. And a female. I think I need a drink."

"Welcome to my world."

"I think I've been welcomed already. Without my permission." She covered her face. "I can't believe this is happening."

Andrus reached over and gently pried one of her hands away so she would meet his eyes and see the truth in them. "There is nothing to fear. I promise."

She gave him a weak little smile and then unexpectedly laced her fingers between his, tightly holding his hand the rest of the drive. He felt surprised by how their hands fit together and even more surprised by the way the heat of her palm simultaneously aroused him.

Again, he'd had to fight off the urge to sample her lips. Because, clearly, she wasn't interested in him that way. And, of course, he was practically spoken for.

Andrus pulled up to a large Spanish-style villa with a circular driveway and cactus garden. Nestled into the Hollywood hills, it overlooked Los Angeles. *Quite the palace.* But no comparison to his castle. *With that thing in the basement that shall never be spoken of.*

"This should be the place." He hadn't been here before, but it was the address Tommaso had texted him.

"Andrus?" Sadie looked at him with her warm brown eyes. "I can't believe I'm about to say this, but I don't want you to leave me. I'm really, really afraid."

Suddenly, something about seeing this woman so vulnerable infuriated him. She was beautiful, intelligent, fearless, and sharp-tongued. *All right, and frustrating and stubborn and quite flippant.* Nevertheless, Tim had harmed her, and it made his blood boil.

He did not like to think of anyone touching her.

Andrus did his best to give her a consoling smile and grabbed her soft little hand again. But the touch wasn't exactly for her benefit. He found himself wanting the contact more than he should.

"You have no reason to be afraid," he said. "Tim will be dealt with, and you will go on with your mortal life to live your dream of becoming an actress."

Her breath hitched. "Oh crap! I have an audition at six." She looked at her watch. "In an hour."

"You cannot go."

"I have to. They called this afternoon before Tim came over. It's for a speaking part in a major movie."

"I am very sorry, but I must track this Tim before he slips away and attacks you again."

She got out of his truck, but instead of walking up to Tommaso's home, she went in the opposite direction down the long driveway.

"Woman, just where the hell do you think you're going?" he bellowed.

She held up her middle finger and kept on walking.

Obstinate woman. And did she have to shake her ass like that while she marched away? The movement made him harder than a rock. Or was it the fact that she'd disobeyed him, and he found her feisty nature extremely fucking titillating?

Stop it, Andrus. You cannot have her. She is to help you prepare to meet your new mate Charlotte in a few days. Still, he wanted to run after Sadie and kiss her again.

He sighed longingly and continued watching that ass shimmy away until it was nearly out of sight.

"Okay," he said under his breath, "time to go retrieve the human." If he was lucky, he'd get her back to the driveway and she'd walk away again.

I could do this all day. Except, he needed to hunt down Tim and they needed to get on with his tutoring.

He gave himself a little pinch to get his head out of his ass and jogged after her, catching up quickly. Even if she were running, she'd be no match for his speed. "Sadie, please be reasonable."

"You don't own me."

But perhaps I would like to possess you. In bed.

No, Andrus. Cease these thoughts immediately. Where had all this come from anyway?

"Correct," he replied. "However, you and I both know I can throw you over my shoulder and force you." *And that I would like the feel of your body riding on mine.*

"Lay one finger on me, and it will be the last time you see your digit."

Oh, silly mortal. She could not injure him. And didn't she know that her prickly tongue was turning him the hell on? She needed to stop immediately or he might do something he regretted.

"I'm giving you one final warning, Sadie. I am trying to help you."

She stopped and looked at him with a scowl on those sweet little plump lips that begged for a kiss.

Yes, kiss her. Look at that mouth. It is perfect for—

"Listen, Andrus, I am grateful that you care. But I can't let this prick derail my plans."

Speaking of prick, he hoped she didn't glance down at his fully aroused cock. "You have no choice. And might I remind you how frightened you were a mere sixty seconds ago, which was the correct response."

She shrugged. "I guess I got over it."

"I'm not letting you go."

"I did *not* ask you to be my bodyguard. I don't even know you. So as far as I'm concerned, you may bite me."

Gods, he couldn't take much more of her cheeky little growls and back talk. It just made him want to fuck her so hard.

"Sadie, I'm sorry to inform you, but you've already been bitten. This is why I must find Tim."

She blinked at him.

"I did not wish to frighten you further," he explained, taking the opportunity to touch her again and placing his hands on her arms, "however, there is a bite mark on the back of your shoulder."

She slapped her hand over the spot. "Oh shit. Am I going to turn into a werewolf or something?"

"Good God, I hope not. You're bitchy enough as it is."

She growled at him.

"What? I was merely jesting. You see how I said 'bitch'? The word for a female dog—oh neverthefuckmind."

The tears began welling in her eyes.

Oh no. Oh no. I hate watching females cry.

"My life is over. I can't believe it," she sobbed.

"Your life isn't over, but I really must find your ex-boyfriend before the trail gets cold. All right?" He reached out and wiped away a tear from under her eye and then gripped her chin, forcing her to meet his gaze. "I promise you, Sexy Sadie, I will help you."

She nodded solemnly. "Thank you, Andrus."

Sadie couldn't believe her goddamned luck. It was bad enough to have been attacked and not remember details that might help Andrus catch this guy, but bitten? And now she'd lose her chance at her big audition, too?

Why the hell me? Why?

This situation gave a whole new meaning to the term loser magnet. She was more like the loser mecca. Oddly, though, the news revealed by Andrus about his true nature didn't really scare her so much. Being an actress, she'd put on so many personalities and characters over the years—elf, mermaid, heiress, Valley girl, businesswoman, giant dildo (for a sex store grand opening)—that sometimes make-believe felt real (except the being a dildo part) and the real world felt like the farce.

That being said, the news about all of these other species hadn't quite sunk in yet. First, there was the fact that he was a demigod and her fucking agent was a goddess! Seriously? She'd always sensed there was something off about that man. Then the other creatures Andrus had mentioned—vampires and those crazy Mayan priests—sounded scary as hell. Worst of all, however, she'd been bitten and she might actually turn into...a something other than human.

L.A. is the worst.

The only thing holding her together right now— and this was the really crazy part—was Andrus. The moment he'd revealed what he truly was, something clicked inside her. Some sort of...she didn't know, really. It simply felt like the blinders had been removed, and now she saw him for who he truly was. After that, she found herself wanting to touch him and be near him.

Must be the stress of the situation. Yes. That's it.

But then why can't I stop thinking about kissing him again? Those pouty bad-boy lips were so irresistible.

She sighed longingly as Andrus rang the doorbell of his friend's home.

"Do not worry, meat wench; all will be well," he said, mistaking her sigh for worry and taking her hand, sending a little wave of tingles through her core.

She caught a discreet smile on his face. He was trying to make her feel better with a little humor. It was very sweet.

"The sad part is," she said, "I'd actually take meat wench over my current status."

The front door swung open, and there stood a beautiful as hell, elegant man with fine facial features, dressed in an expensive black suit and deep purple tie. His height was a few inches shorter than Andrus—about six two or so—and his build was considerably leaner, but he was drop-dead gorgeous. The turquoise eyes were especially stunning against his olive skin.

Wow. If Andrus was the poster child for sexy, ripped tough guys, Tommaso was the poster boy for male models everywhere.

"Well, well. Who do we have here?" Tommaso said, in a smooth accented voice. It wasn't Eastern European like Andrus. Italian perhaps?

"Cut the crap, Tommy," Andrus said. "This is Sadie. Sadie, this is little Tommy."

Tommy ignored Andrus and smiled at her. "You may call me Tommaso like everyone else in the world who doesn't have brain damage from overexposure to crazy vampire blood." He reached for her hand and kissed the top. "It's a pleasure to meet you."

Andrus growled.

Had he just gotten jealous? The thought sent a spike of excited flutters through her stomach.

"Won't you come in?" Tommaso offered.

"Thanks." She stepped into the foyer and Andrus followed. The interior looked like a Mediterranean paradise with raised ceilings and several huge potted palm trees that reached the enormous skylights.

"Wow," she said. "What a lovely home."

"Thank you," Tommaso replied. "It is a recent purchase for my bride-to-be."

"Oh. You're engaged?" she asked.

"Not yet. But just as soon as I meet her." He winked.

Weird.

Tommaso showed them to the kitchen—about ten times the size of her shoe-box apartment—and made her an espresso, while Andrus told him the details of what he'd seen in her apartment.

"Well," Tommaso said, placing a lemon peel on the edge of her little white cup with his elegant fingers, "my guess is it's a vampire."

"No," Andrus said. "The smell was...different. Familiar, yet strangely not."

Tommaso shrugged and placed the little cup in front of her. It smelled delicious. And the way Tommaso handled himself reminded her of James Bond—a gentleman with a few hidden sharp edges. *Probably some weapons, too.*

"Thank you," she said.

He dipped his head. "It's my pleasure, Sadie. May I offer you a biscotti? I baked them myself this morning."

"God, you're adorable," she said. "And you smell so nice."

She heard a little grunt to her side from Andrus.

Had he just gotten jealous again? *No. I'm sure I'm misreading him. He doesn't even like me.* Although, he was going out of his way to make her feel protected.

"You smell nice, too," she said to Andrus. "And I bet you'd smell even better if you took a shower and stopped brushing with whisky." Not that she found his smell offensive. Quite the contrary. He had a very masculine scent, like leather and a little sweat and maybe some evaporating alcohol. It wasn't bad at all, but she could probably smell more of his addictive scent if he made an effort. "I thought you smelled damned nice the night you attacked me," she offered.

"He attacked you?" Tommaso asked, smirking.

"I was trying to serve him steak at this table, Brazilian style."

"I love *churrascaria*," Tommaso said. "It is one of my favorite styles of dining for dates."

"I know, right?" she agreed.

"Well, if you two girls will excuse me, I have an evil victimizer of the weak and helpless to pursue."

"Who are you calling weak and helpless?" she asked. Did he really think that of her? Jesus. She was anything but. In fact, being independent and taking care of herself was something she prided herself on. It seriously irked her to know that he thought so little of her.

"I am merely pointing out the truth: Humans are fragile," Andrus replied. "It is why other species enjoy feeding on you; you're simply lower in the food chain."

Her jaw dropped open. "So I'm a chicken or a goat?" Wow, just when she was starting to like him.

"You're a human," he replied. "However, the analogy is correct, which is why you need me."

Like hell I do! "I think it's time for you to go before this chick pecks out your eyes."

"Such big words for such a frail little creature," Andrus said.

"Oh, my friend. What a way you have with the ladies." Tommaso chuckled.

Andrus gave Tommaso the death stare and left without another word.

"God." She shook her head. "I don't get that man. One minute he's so sweet, and the next he's such a...barbarian."

"It might seem that way at first glance," Tommaso said with that smooth, charming accent. "However, deep down inside, Andrus is nothing but a big puppy from another time. Except if you're an evil vampire or some other sort of despicable creature. Then he's as lethal as they come. The rest of the time, though, he's usually trying to hide his true nature: a big man with a big heart and huge soft spot for helping people. Especially loves kids. He's also as loyal as they come," Tommaso added.

"So why does he act like..." she waved her hand in the direction of the front door, "like that?"

"He's had his heart stomped on a few times, and when that happens, most of us put up walls. His just happens to be made of antiquated chauvinism and swords. But he's really a good guy. I promise."

Darnit. Now she felt terrible for snapping at him. Probably because she knew Tommaso was right. Andrus had shown up to her apartment, saw something was going on, and jumped right in to help her. He didn't ask for anything in return. She just wished he wouldn't treat her like she was less than him.

Why the hell is it bothering me so much? She barely knew the guy. Yet...in the space of less than one day, she suddenly felt herself wondering where he'd been all her life. It was the strangest damned thing, but something about him felt so...good.

"I'll be right back," she said, hoping to catch him before he left.

CHAPTER ELEVEN

Andrus was not happy. Not even a little. He was going out of this way to help this female, yet did she show him any gratitude?

"Oh, no. You smell great, Tommaso," he mimicked in his best whiny female voice. "I love your suit. Oh, espresso! Yummy." He punched a few key words into his cell, still sitting in Tommaso's driveway.

Vagina art. Talking vaginas. Walking vaginas.

As his phone did its thing, searching for vagina-themed art exhibitions, he continued his little Sadie-toned rant. "You're an asshole. Bite me. I'm a strong woman and need no one."

"Eh-hem," said a female voice, through the lowered window at his side.

Andrus jumped in his seat, finding Sadie standing there with a huge scowl on her face.

"Do not sneak up on me, woman! Men like me decapitate first, ask questions later."

She folded her arms over her chest, causing her breasts to plump. *Damn, they look so soft and squeezable and—*

"I came out here to say thank you for helping me and that I was sorry for what I said. But now, I just want to punch your nose."

"My apologies, Sadie, but you are very—"

"Weak?" She rolled her eyes. "Andrus, you can't go around being such a racist just because you're built a little stronger than the rest of us."

Nice to know she's come to grips with the truth so quickly.

"The correct term would be species-ists," he said, "as a race is defined as a group of humans who share a distinct set of similar physical traits. Species is a classification to separate a genus. However, I was about to say confusing. That said, I cannot help that you are in need of assistance to survive."

"Uh-huh. Welp, Mr. Perfect, may I remind you that I was hired to help you first. I believe it had something to do with your lack of social skills? And, by the way, I can see we're going to have to start with the basics. One of which is not acting like a giant, Neanderthal jackass. What is with you anyway?"

"Oh, so you believe I should behave like Tommaso?"

"It wouldn't hurt. At least he doesn't act like he's the gods' gift to humanity."

Sadie had unknowingly pushed his biggest button. He'd been forced to sacrifice everything he was, everything he had for the benefit of humans. For three hundred years he lived in misery, killing, protecting, and doing everything in his power not to lose his sanity. And when it was all over, did he seek revenge or spend his time hating the gods who'd enslaved him and his men? No. He was too damned happy to be free again to waste his time on crying about it, but he would never tolerate anyone ever belittling him or judging him.

It especially stung coming from this woman, although he didn't know why.

He hopped from the car because this message deserved a little face-to-face growling. "Please explain to me, oh mighty human, how having such chivalrous skills would have made me a more efficient hunter of the very species that sought to make you their food slaves? Explain to me how wearing a suit or using the right fork or paying a lady pleasant compliments would have assisted me in slaying over ten thousand bloodthirsty bastards or helped me to lead my men? All of whom were enslaved by the gods to do horrible, grueling work, without a say or any hope of freedom, the threat of our families' safety or eternal damnation held over our heads? Explain why a man who has had everything he ever loved taken, killed, or destroyed would give a fucking rat's ass about silk ties or tasty coffee—okay, the coffee, yes—I'm not a barbarian, after all—but other than that? No."

Sadie stared up at him with her big, honey-brown eyes, her expression unreadable. "I guess I'd say that you did a really, really good thing and probably no one ever thanked you. So, coming from one of the people who benefited from your sacrifice, thank you. I really mean that. But if, like you said, those horrible things are all gone, don't you owe it to yourself to move on? To have a life? Re-enter civilization? I can see the bitterness in your eyes, Andrus. You're not happy. And you deserve to be."

He scratched the back of his head and swallowed. "Perhaps you have a point."

She smiled warmly and placed her hand on his whiskered cheek. Once again the intimacy of the gesture sparked something deep inside him. It was a feeling of...of...

Happiness?

"Then let me help you," she said. "It's only right, considering what you're doing for me."

He didn't know what to say. He'd never accepted help from anyone. He was always the one who got leaned on, did the dirty work, made the sacrifices. But receive help?

"Please?" she said sweetly.

"Why?" he asked.

"Because there's something in my gut that tells me you're worth the effort."

Andrus's little rant had given Sadie a glimpse of something she hadn't expected: The truth about the person he really was.

It all makes so much sense now.

He wasn't a chauvinistic a-hole—not exactly—but he was a man who'd lived in a constant state of warfare for over three hundred years. He'd been so disconnected from the world, his social views simply hadn't evolved with the times. And now, she couldn't really fault him for anything.

"Why do you think you know how to help me?" he asked.

A complicated question. But when she was about five, her parents divorced and her father got custody. It was something they said would make everyone happy, and being just a child, she didn't understand how being separated from her mother would do anything but make her sad. That was the point in her life when she began developing her skills as an actress. Because her father was sad, too. All the time. So she did her best to hide the fact that she missed her mother, instead focusing on being there for her father. His source of cheer. Eventually, her father remarried a nice woman, Lauren, who Sadie and her sister considered to be their mother because Lauren was the one who raised them, cared for them, prepared their lunches, and made their father smile again. Her real mother, though? Who knew? She sent a postcard every few years at first. Sometimes she'd send a book or trinket, but those ended up in the trash. Thinking of her mother only made her feel sad, rejected, though she never let it show. Then after the age of ten, her mother stopped sending anything at all.

It took her a very, very long time to understand that she had to stop feeling like she'd done something wrong or wasn't good enough for her mother, but that was how acting had helped. She'd gotten to try on different people and situations, to safely explore her vastly conflicted emotions. It helped her let go and move on.

So, if anything, she knew she could help Andrus do the same. Maybe it was the real reason they'd been brought together. Regardless, something about him felt so irresistible. Especially when he showed that sweet sexy side he tried to hide.

"Well," she finally replied, "how do *you* know you can help me with my problems?"

"Experience," he replied, beaming with confidence in those smoldering turquoise-blue eyes.

"Same here, big man." And then something came over her. It was one of those kiss first, ask questions later impulses.

She pushed herself up on her toes, threw her arms around his neck, and kissed him. *Ohgods.* The heat of his lips had an immediate reaction. Mainly, throbbing between her legs.

He slid his arms around her waist and pulled her in closer, opening his mouth in reply to her bold intrusion. The kiss suddenly became a teasing dance of their tongues, both of them seeming to take a moment to feel and taste the other.

Despite her earlier comments, he tasted nothing like whisky. More like honey and fresh mint.

So delicious.

She felt her entire body melt into him, heating from head to curling toes. The way his lips kneaded her mouth—not too smooth or rehearsed, but filled with raw lust and unabashed need—the way he held her to his hard body with his powerful arms, the way her nipples hardened and goose bumps erupted on every inch of her body, all felt more raw and sexual than any sex she'd ever had.

As she clung to his muscular towering body, getting instantly wet for him and relishing the sinful sexual energy flowing between their tightly pressed bodies, his cock grew hard against her stomach.

Oh, lord. She wanted to touch that giant bulge again, but this time without the leather. She wanted him naked and on top of her, nestled between her warm thighs like that first night they'd met.

Wait. What am I doing?

Uh, you're making out with Andrus in some guy's driveway.

Oh shit. She pulled away and the look on his face was pure cockiness—full-blown smirk on his wet lips.

"Ah, you see," he said. "You do find me irresistible, but I am a man of my word and promised not to judge you for lying about it earlier."

She huffed and turned away. "That was a pity kiss!" she called out, now feeling embarrassed.

"I'll see you later. After I'm done saving your life again!" he screamed back, laughing.

She entered Tommaso's home and pressed her back against the closed door, letting out a whoosh. That had been one hell of a kiss, but who was she kidding? She could never be happy with a man like that. Not even if she managed to help him. Sure, he might have his attractive qualities—stunning eyes, hypnotic deep voice, raw masculinity, and witty, addictive cockiness—but he definitely wasn't relationship material. At least not for her. He would never see her as his equal. That he'd made perfectly clear.

Yeah, but you still need to help him. Yes, they could be friends, and she'd tell him so the moment he returned.

CHAPTER TWELVE

Just before nine in the evening, Andrus pulled up to the third Malibu art gallery on his list. Frankly, it was shocking the number of exhibits he'd found with talking vaginas. In his day, such a scandalous thing was unheard of. If you wanted to converse with a woman's private parts, you had to get married. Women's bodies were sacred, meant to be cherished and protected. And a man's job was to do the cherishing and protecting. Did that mean casual sex was off the table? Hell no. But it did mean if you took a woman to bed, you'd better pleasure her properly, leaving her limp and exhausted and thoroughly worked over from head to toe. Frankly, there was nothing casual about it.

Hard, hard work and dedication.

Suddenly, an image of Sadie with her auburn hair spread over a pillow, her naked body laid out beneath him, popped into his head. Then he thought of that kiss. Soft and luscious, the kind of kiss that sparks a man's soul to life as well as his cock.

He looked down at his leather pants and adjusted himself once again. Would his dick ever stop being so hard? *Not until you do something about it.*

He sighed. It was five days to go until the party. If his second-chance mate truly showed, he'd be giving her one hell of a night.

The thought of Sadie's kiss hit him again.

Oh, hell. What if she's really beginning to like me? Not likely, but he was a man of honor and would have to tell her the truth. There could be nothing between them. Because if this Charlotte was who Cimil said, he'd want his mate and no one else. Then they'd have a son and that would be that.

I'll tell Sadie as soon as I see her. It was just that he really enjoyed the feel of her in his arms. *Maybe I will kiss her one more time before I break the news.*

He hopped from his Hummer, which he'd parked in the back lot of the gallery, and entered around the front, hoping to get in before they closed.

There were no talking vaginas inside, but the smell was the same as what he'd found in Sadie's apartment, though very, very faint.

"May I help you, sir?" said a young blonde from behind a desk in the corner.

"I am looking for Tim."

"Oh, he didn't come in today. Can I help you find something in particular? Right now we are featuring the Orozco collection. He's a Mexican artist who paints spirit animals."

Andrus flashed a quick glance at one of the

paintings on the wall of a duck with porcupine quills. "While that is an excellent duckupine, I'm afraid I'm only here to see Tim. Any idea when he'll be in or where I may find him?"

She shook her head. "Honestly, no. I called earlier today, but he's not answering."

The SOB probably returned to Sadie's apartment and sensed me. Demigods didn't have a particular scent like other species, but they did leave behind a sort of energy. If Tim got wind of him, he might be on the run.

"But," she added, "I didn't try his home phone. Give me a minute." She dug out a small address book from her purse and dialed. After a few moments she looked up at him and shook her head. "He's not answering there, either. But if you leave your name and number, I'm sure he'll arrange a private viewing of anything you'd like to see."

"On second thought, I am in the market for a new piece for my living room. Have anything with swords?"

She held up her finger. "I think Tim still has some paintings from the medieval torture show. I'll go check." She got up and disappeared into the back.

Andrus went for her phone book, found Tim's home address, and placed the book back inside her bag. Moments later, she emerged carrying a large canvas depicting a knight in armor stabbing a unicorn with fangs.

"Sorry. This was the only one I could find," she said. "It's by a local artist who's just starting out, so the price is very reasonable."

"Oh, that's perfect. I'll take it."

A few hours later, Andrus pulled up to Tommaso's house. His hunt for Tim had been a complete bust. The man had not been at home, and not wanting to alarm him, Andrus decided not to break in to search the place. It was a better option to come back later and see if Tim returned. However, just in case the guy had decided to take his show on the road, he gave Cimil and Zac a heads-up to warn the gods and their Uchben. Uchben were the humans who worked for the gods in every capacity imaginable: warriors, accountants, doctors, teachers, bankers, you name it. There wasn't a country or city on the planet that didn't have the Uchben embedded into their infrastructure. It was the only way for so few deities to keep the wheels on the humanity bus, so to speak. And in exchange for being the eyes and ears of the gods, the Uchben were compensated with considerable perks: free education, 401(k), dental and medical. Those who were deemed indispensable were gifted with the light of the gods—immortality—such was the case for the leaders of the army.

In any case, they'd now been alerted that there was an immortal out there attacking innocent humans. A considerable no-no. However, that did not eliminate the threat, so he had to come up with some other way to keep her safe until Tim was caught.

Now almost midnight, Andrus rang Tommaso's doorbell, but no one answered. "What the holy fuck?"

Panic set in. What if this creature had found her? He went around to the side window and looked in. He could only view into the dimly lit dining room and part of the kitchen, but nothing seemed disturbed.

He dialed Tommaso's cell, who answered after several rings. "Hey, Andrus buddy! There you are." Loud music and laughter in the background told him they were at a club or a bar.

"You took her out to party?" Andrus growled. "What the hell is the matter with you?"

"What? I can't hear you. But yeah, you should come join us. We're at the Randy Unicorn! I'll text you the address."

The Randy Unicorn?

He was about to tell Tommaso to bring Sadie the fuck back, but Tommaso bellowed, "My cell is almost out of juice, man. See you soon!" He hung up.

A second later, an address popped up. Andrus texted back: *Going to skin you alive. Bring her back to your house.*

The message bounced back.

What kind of idiot takes a woman who's being hunted by God-only-knows-what out for a night on the town? He was going to kick the crap out of his comrade just as soon as he got Sadie somewhere safe.

Forty minutes later—*godsdamned traffic!*—Andrus arrived at the Randy Unicorn. He pulled up to the valet and noted the long line of mortals dressed as unicorns of every imaginable sort—Goth unicorn, Elvis unicorn, werebear unicorn. Nothing like the real thing. *Thank gods for that.* Real unicorns were terrifying.

He stood at the red rope, waiting for the bouncer to let him in, but after ten seconds, his patience wore out. He unlatched the rope and headed for the door. The bouncer, a large mortal male wearing a crocheted unicorn beanie that had obviously been forced upon him, held out his hand. "Hey, where do you think you're going, man?"

Andrus turned to face him, looked down at the man's offending hand, and growled.

The guy snapped his hand back. "Okay, no need to get nasty. But you do need to wear something unicorn. Like a hat or T-shirt or something, man." He pointed to the little display case right inside, filled with all sorts of unicorn crap, including strap-on light-up horns.

"Have you ever seen a unicorn?" Andrus snarled.

The man shook his head stiffly.

"Well, neither have I, but I hear that if they ever show themselves to you, one look will liquefy your innards and make you bleed from your eye sockets. Then they use that horn to impale you from the rectum and drink your insides, using their horn like a giant fucking straw, while you remain awake for the entire event, screaming in agony."

He turned his head to a young woman standing there listening. She wore a "Time to be a Unicorn" T-shirt.

"You fucking sure about that, honey?" he asked and then pushed past the bouncer inside, where he couldn't quite believe his eyes.

Hell is a real place.

Couldn't Tommaso have at least chosen a more respectable establishment like a leather daddy bar? (He'd gone to one with Helena once.) At least those gay men had good taste in music and knew how to dress properly. *This place is like dying a thousand deaths per second.* Fucking neon glow-in-the dark rainbows everywhere—on the chairs, tables, and walls. Even the floors were painted with fluffy clouds and strips of color that illuminated in the dark with the black lights.

I stand corrected. This is far worse than hell.

He made his way through the packed dance floor, catching curious looks from the crowd who were dressed as...*yeah, you fucking guessed it: unicorns.* Finally, he spotted Tommaso at the bar. He wore a dark tailored suit and was speaking to a young woman wearing a sort of rainbow jumpsuit.

"You have some fucking explaining to do, Tommaso!" Andrus barked over the music.

Tommaso smiled coolly. "Nice to see you, too. What's got your leather panties in a tangle? Not digging the unicorn vibe?" He ripped open his blazer to reveal a very lame and girly-looking T-shirt that read: *Unicorns Make Me Horny.*

Andrus scowled. "Nice. Real nice. I'll deal with you later. Where the fuck is Sadie?"

"She's dancing right..." He pointed to a spot on the dance floor where Sadie obviously wasn't dancing. "Fuck. She was right there. I swear it."

Andrus was going to kill Tommaso. But first, he had to find Sadie.

Taller than the humans, minus their horns, Andrus's eyes went to work, scanning the floor. "I don't see her."

"I'll check the bathrooms," Tommaso said. "You see if she went out the back."

Andrus charged through the crowd, pushing his way toward a door that likely led to some back office and storage. As soon as the door opened, the smell hit him. It was Tim or whatever the hell its name was.

"Sadie!" he called, following the scent toward another door. He pushed it open and stumbled out into the back alley. Sadie lay face down on the cement.

Oh shit. No, no, no. He rushed to her side and carefully flipped her over. Blood and scratches covered her face and arms.

His heart fell into a tailspin of rage. He placed his ear to her chest. *Thank gods, she's not dead.* But clearly this thing had fed on her again. There was a fresh bite mark on her hand.

"Oh fuck! Is she okay?" Tommaso said from the doorway.

"No. She's not okay, asshole." Andrus scooped Sadie into his arms. "But you're going to be," he whispered. "You're going to be."

Sadie's eyes cracked open. "Andrus?" Her voice was barely audible. "What happened?"

"Fucking Tim. That's what happened. But I won't let him touch you again."

CHAPTER THIRTEEN

Sadie awoke on a to-die-for-comfortable, king-sized bed. From the soft glow of sunlight through the khaki-gray curtains it was obviously daytime. *Where the hell am I?* she wondered.

The last thing she recalled was being at that club with Tommaso and dancing with some shirtless guy in a rainbow afro wig.

She slowly sat up, gripping the sides of her head. "Owww..." *I definitely remember doing tequila shots.*

She stumbled from the bed and found the bathroom, a huge, modern, white-marble spa. Whose home was this? Tommaso's, she guessed.

She washed her face and used some mouthwash she found under the sink to rinse away the foul taste of salt and whatever else was left over from a night of Lick-Sip-Sucks (salt, shot, lime wedge).

She then looked up in the mirror and saw scratches on her face. "Jesus." There were more on her arms and a bite mark on her hand.

"Ah, I see our party princess is awake." Andrus stood in the doorway, wearing a clean white tee and faded jeans that hung low on his hips, accentuating his broad shoulders and lean torso.

The smell of freshly washed man filled the bathroom.

"The showered look works well for you," she grumbled. He'd even trimmed his black beard down to a sexy scruff.

"Yes, you inspired me to turn over a more civilized leaf. Although, I still find underwear far too constricting." He shrugged. "I hear commando is back in style anyways."

She made a little laugh that felt like having hot branding irons shoved through her skull. "Owww..." she moaned, stumbling to one side. "I don't feel so good—it's because that thing attacked me again, isn't it?" Or maybe because she'd attacked the bottle? In her defense, yesterday had been one hell of a day.

Andrus grabbed her gently by the shoulders. "Perhaps we should get some nourishment into you first. Right this way, I've prepared breakfast."

He walked her through a well-lit living room with raised ceilings and gleaming blond hardwood floors. "Where are we?" she asked. It wasn't Tommaso's place.

"Eat first. Then I'll explain everything." He showed her into a large kitchen with a breakfast bar in the center island. The cupboards were made of those little French-style doors with clear glass that she loved, and all of the appliances looked brand new.

On the counter was one setting, a glass of

orange juice, a bowl of fresh berries and some cereal.

"Sorry, I don't actually know how to cook," he said.

"No. This is wonderful, thank you." She climbed into the chair and looked at him. "What happened last night?"

"I wanted to ask you the same question," he replied, leaning against the sink, crossing his insanely thick arms over his massively chiseled pecs.

She popped a blackberry into her mouth and chewed. "I don't know. Tommaso volunteered to take me to my audition—which went great, by the way; the director totally seemed like he wanted to give me the part—then we went out to celebrate."

"I told you not to leave his house," Andrus said.

"It was his idea. Besides, he said he's a retired Ukleen or Ukwad or—"

"Uchben. They are servants of the gods. He was once a soldier for them. Nevertheless, you must start listening to me. Whatever this thing is, it's dangerous. Now tell me, what's the last thing you remember?"

"I don't know. I was dancing with this guy and then…" She rubbed her eyes. "I kind of remember my head hurting and then I woke up here."

"Did you see Tim?"

She shook her head. "No."

"But I smelled him there. Are you sure?" he asked.

"Yeah. I never saw him."

"He must've snuck up behind you and taken you outside."

I feel so violated. This was honestly freaking her the hell out. *I think I'm going to be sick.*

"How is he doing this to me?" she asked. "How does he make me forget everything?"

"Some species—vampires, for example—have the ability to glamour humans and make them forget seeing things. They can also implant suggestions. It's possible that Tim has this ability and glamoured someone to lure you outside to the alley where I found you."

"Oh God." She dropped her head into her hands. "He's trying to turn me into something, isn't he? It's like the three bites rule."

Andrus came over and began rubbing her back, instantly making her feel a little better. It was strange how he had that effect, like she somehow absorbed emotions from him.

"Species who are able to infect others can generally do so with one bite," he said, "which is why I'm beginning to think he merely wishes to feed on you for a while."

She held back her tears. "Well, I'm not going to let him ruin my life." She'd come to L.A. to live her dream.

"I won't allow that either; however, until he's

caught, you will need to stay here."

"Here?" she asked.

"Yes. I've rented this home for you. It has twenty-four-hour armed security, state-of-the-art alarm system, and one extremely vicious, well-trained cocker spaniel outside."

She shot him a look. Was he out of his mind?

He shrugged. "Okay, he's not trained, but I thought the dog might be good company. And I do believe I can teach Niccolo to warn you if there are snacks in the vicinity."

"Niccolo is the dog?"

"Nick, for short."

Okay. Whatever. "Andrus, I really, really appreciate this, but I can't accept."

"If it's about the expense, I assure you that—"

"No. It's not about that, although I'm definitely wondering how an unemployed ex-assassin makes a living, but it's about me being a prisoner."

"Protection is not prison. And it's either this or let Tim continue feeding on you until he grows bored and finishes you off. Or turns you into whatever he is, if he's one of those contagion-based species. If not, then he just wants to eat you. Until you're dead." He shrugged casually.

She sighed. She didn't want to die, but this?

"Besides, you still haven't completed your work with me," he said.

She laughed. "You're not even an actor. And now that you bring it up, I've been wanting to ask why I was even hired for you."

"Yes, about that. I've been meaning to tell you something."

"Okay?" She didn't like the serious tone of his voice.

"The reason Cimil, aka Bob, hired you was to prepare me for an event in four days. She thought it best I show up armed with a few extra tools in the charm department."

Honestly, his unpolished, barbaric ways were beginning to grow on her, which might have something to do with the fact she couldn't stop thinking about that kiss from yesterday. In fact—and despite the issue of him not being relationship material—maybe it wouldn't hurt to hole up for a few days with Andrus and repeat the kiss a few times just to make sure she hadn't imagined how good it was. Especially now that he smelled all fresh and clean and had on those sexy jeans that hung just so low on his trim waist.

"What kind of event?" she asked.

"I am to be introduced to my new mate."

Sadie felt like the floor had dropped out from under her. *Mate?* "You mean...?"

"In my world, a mate is like a wife, only the Universe has selected her. And once mates find and accept each other, there can be no other."

"Oh," was the only thing she could manage to say.

How about saying you're an idiot. A complete

idiot. Her oddly unexpected interest in him was a one-way street.

"Ummm...congratulations.   That   sounds wonderful." She got up from the chair. "I think I'll go take a shower now."

"Sadie, I meant to tell you, but there wasn't really time and—"

"No, no." She held out her hand. "You don't owe me any explanation. Like I said, yesterday was only a pity kiss." She headed back through the living room toward her room.

"There are clean clothes for you in the closet," he offered, his voice full of apology.

I'm such an idiot. I'm such an idiot. "Thanks! That was very thoughtful."

Now, she definitely needed to get the hell out of there.

Andrus wondered why that had been so difficult. He barely knew Sadie, but telling her about his mate felt like a betrayal.

He blew out a grumbly breath. *What the hell is wrong with me?* He obviously felt an attraction for Sadie—she was, after all, very sexy—and he did feel extremely protective over her, too. Nevertheless, she'd been hired to help him achieve the goal of charming his new mate.

Eh, yeah. Which might all be a hoax. Dammit.

Come to think of it, this mounting tension and guilt still smelled suspiciously of a Cimil plot. *She probably wishes Sadie to fall in love with me and then have me break her heart when I meet this other woman.* Yes, that certainly sounded like something the crazy goddess would do. *I need to speak with Cimil and get the truth.*

He slipped his cell from his pants and called the office. A lovely female voice answered. "Immortal Matchmakers. This is Tula speaking. How may I help you?"

"Tula, good morning. This is Andrus Gray. I must speak with Cimil. Is she available?"

"Yes. She is expecting your call. One moment, please."

Of course she is. Which means she already knows the outcome of all this.

"Andrus!" Cimil's voice came on the line. "What a surprise."

"Funny, Cimil. Tula said you were waiting for my call, which means you know what I want."

"Yes."

A long, long, looong moment of silence passed.

"Well?" Andrus growled.

"Who's this?" Cimil asked.

"Andrus. Don't fuck with me."

"Andrus Dontfuckwithme? I don't think I know you."

He sighed with a groan. "Cimil, it is me: Andrus Gray. Now tell me the godsdamned truth; is my new mate really going to be at the party?"

"Ah! Andrus! Yes, I told you already: her name is Charlotte, and she is very excited to meet you. How is the man-ners class coming? Get it? Manners? You're a man—damn, I crack myself up."

"So she really exists?" he asked.

"Yes."

"Swear to me, Cimil. Swear that you are not lying to me."

"I swear on my unborn babies' lives that I am not lying to you."

"You're pregnant again?" Universe help them all.

"No, but I will be. And don't tell Roberto. He might burn himself at the stake if he found out. Can you believe an ancient Egyptian vampire says he can't handle the four we have? I mean, the man doesn't require sleep, but you'd think he was mortal with all of the 'Oh, I'm so tireds' and the 'Oh, why are they so needys?' Just wait until I crank out the next batch of four."

"Cimiiil?" he growled. Why did she always have to try to distract people with her random mental vomit and frightening drama?

"What?" she said. "The man begged me for children. So now he's gettin' his own small tribe— my reproductive years are far from over—I've got at least another good...eternity in me. How many kids do you think I could make in an eternity?"

Oh, demons of death and destruction. Please

stop this insane goddess from procreating any more evil offspring. "I mean that you should return to our conversation at hand."

"What were we talking about?"

Poke out my eye. Someone please just poke it. "About my mate, Charlotte, and you swearing that she is who you say."

"Oh. Are we talking about that again?"

"Just tell me; if she is my mate, then why do I have feelings for this Sadie?"

"How the hell should I know? What do I look like, an all-knowing goddess?"

I hate you. I truly hate you. "Can you at least tell me what this creature is who hunts her?"

"Ah, yes! The creature. No," she replied.

"What?" She'd completely lost him.

"Yes. The creature who hunts her. No."

Going to kill her. Really, really going to kill her. "Cimil, what is the creature?"

"I just told you; I don't know. I see no creature hunting her."

"So if you cannot see it, does that mean it's using Maaskab-like tricks?" The Maaskab concealed themselves from the gods for centuries by slathering their bodies in black jade paste. Black jade was also the same material used to blunt a deity's power. "In fact, could this creature be an actual Maaskab?"

"Hmmm..." Cimil said. "It's a possibility. And it would explain why my goddess radar isn't picking anything up."

"I thought you killed them all," he said.

"Oh, no. We left a few alive. One never knows when you'll need an evil Mayan priest adept at the arts of manipulating dark energy, creating tablets and spells used for time travel, and obsessed with enslaving humankind for ritual blood sacrifice. Yanno what I mean?"

"No. Not really."

"In fact, now that you mention it, I do believe we had a Maaskab fill out an online profile."

"What? Are you fucking with me, Cimil?"

"Hold on." He heard Cimil clacking away on her computer. "Here it is. Says he's a Maaskab, never been married or in a serious relationship apart from the Lord of Darkness, and enjoys long walks in puddles of human blood and the smell of destitution."

"What a catch."

"You'd be surprised how many ladies in L.A. would go for this sort of thing."

What the fuck? "He's here in Los Angeles?"

"Yep. But he didn't give an address. Just says to call his cell."

"A Maaskab has a cell? What the hell is this world coming to?"

"Hey, even evil psychotic, bloodthirsty priests need to keep in touch with friends."

"So aren't you going to kill him?" Andrus asked.

"Who?"

"The fucking Maaskab," he replied.

"No, silly. I told you. We only left a few alive, and we might need them one day."

But this had to be the bastard who was feeding off of Sadie. Only Maaskab didn't feed; they just liked to kill or manipulate dark energy. But whatever he was doing to Sadie, he couldn't allow it.

"Fine. Then I will hunt him down and kill him. Give me his number."

"Are you so sure he's the one you're after?" Cimil asked.

"Are you telling me you know something?"

"I know everything. Except the things I don't know, but since I don't know them, then I know everything as far as I'm concerned."

That made no fucking sense.

"The number, Cimil," he demanded.

"Sorry. No can do. We have a strict policy about sharing our clients' personal information."

All right. Now he knew for certain that the goddess was toying with him. "Thanks for nothing, Cimil."

"Always here to serve my fellow immortals. See you at the mixer!"

The call ended and Andrus groaned and rubbed his face. A Maaskab was loose in L.A. and the gods—or at least Cimil—didn't want to do a thing about it.

At least now I know what I'm dealing with. But why the hell would a Maaskab be after Sadie? And how would he catch it?

Hell, I can handle taking down one Maaskab. But as he thought this through, it made less and less sense.

A Maaskab owning an art museum? And walking around in everyday clothing?

Maaskab didn't really wear clothing unless one were to count those loincloths made of human skin and the human finger necklaces they so loved. Then there was the preference for not bathing. Ever. As in never ever, ever, ever. And they slathered themselves in the blood of their victims. The stench was recognizable from ten miles away.

And don't even get me started on their hair. Long black ropes of blood-caked dreads often beaded with human teeth. Their eyes were generally blood-red pits and their mouths dripped with black-whatever likely resulting from the ritualistic crap they ate.

And, because many of them were actually fathered by the God of Male Virility, Chaam, when he'd been going through an evil rough patch, many were just as large as dear old Daddy. Basically seven feet tall, but thankfully without real powers except for the skills they cultivated on their own.

No. Something about this situation wasn't sitting

right. A Maaskab wouldn't be running around L.A. and going unnoticed.

Unless...he's working the next Insidious *movie?*

No. Even they have better standards.

CHAPTER FOURTEEN

Sadie began to sort through the selection of clothing Andrus had brought from her studio apartment and determined that every item she owned was in the walk-in closet.

"What the heck?" she whispered, scratching the back of her wet head of freshly washed hair. She wasn't so sure she liked the idea of Andrus having gone through her stuff, but the gesture was really sweet; he'd wanted her to be comfortable.

And don't forget safe. He seemed to care about her—a practical stranger—and that's why she couldn't stay angry at the man regarding the bomb he'd dropped: He was almost engaged. But they weren't in any sort of relationship, and just because she found the man sexy, in a very brutish sort of way, didn't mean she was really, really into him or had any claim on the guy.

That said, she did owe him. Quite a lot, actually. So if he needed her help to impress this woman, she would do her best to chivalrize him, Prince Charming-ize him, or whatever.

She threw on her favorite pair of jeans and light blue tee and found Andrus sitting in the den. It was empty but for a desk, chair, and laptop.

"Hi. Whatcha doin' there?" she asked.

His turquoise eyes flashed up from the screen. "Looking for something. By the way, how tall was Tim?"

"Uhh... I don't know. Six four or five maybe?"

"How about his hair?" he asked.

"Long, black," she shrugged, "he usually wore it back with a little leather tie. Why?"

"I'm doing some research. Can you tell me anything unusual about him? Tattoos, what he liked to eat, clothing or music preferences?"

"He had some tribal snake tattoos on his back. Nothing else unusual about him except..."

Oh, she really, really didn't want to tell Andrus about the time she'd had sex with Tim. It was pretty strange. And personal.

"What?"

"I'm not sure I want to share this with you."

"I need to find him and definitely need to figure out if he's some sort of Maaskab—or perhaps a slave to a Maaskab. I don't know."

"You can't be serious? You think he's some Mayan witch doctor?"

"Or a minion of sorts. And before you ask, I am not referring to those annoying little one-eyed yellow things on all of the billboards around town."

"Thank God. I'd hate to turn into one of those."

"Agreed. Because then I would have to kill you."

She gave him a terrified look.

"I'm merely joking, Sadie. Even if you turned out to be something so heinous, I would not harm you.

But anything you can tell me about Tim might assist me in tracking him down."

Oh, God. "It's sort of embarrassing."

Andrus stood, walked around to the front of the desk, and leaned against it with those big arms crossed over his big chest. "Trust me, I'm over three hundred years old and my previous mate used to glamour me into submission and then make me watch while she did whatever she liked."

Sadie gasped and covered her mouth. "Oh God, that sounds awful."

He lifted a brow. "I am grateful that my time with her was before the invention of vibrators and nipple clamps. Though, she did find a certain degree of fascination with vegetables."

"On you? She used them on you?"

"No. Thankfully. She liked to make me watch, though. I think it is why I have an aversion to salads." He shrugged. "In any case," he stepped forward and gripped her shoulders, "there is little that can shock me."

She took a deep breath and gazed into his soothing blue eyes. *I swear, there's just something about him that makes me all gooey and hot and bothered and—*

"Any day now, human."

She glared at him. *And such a bossy pig.* "Fine, but lean down. It'll be easier if I whisper it in your ear."

He smirked. "Very well. I am leaning."

She put her mouth to his ear and began to whisper the things that Tim had done to her that one night they'd been together, starting with how he stripped off her clothes and bathed her in a warm bubble bath, caressing her breasts and touching her between her legs. "And once I was warmed up, he took me into the bedroom and turned me around and fucked me from behind. Really, really hard. It wasn't bad, but the entire time, he kept saying that he wanted me to eat him."

Andrus pulled back, his face flushed red.

"Are you okay?" she asked.

"Yea-yeah." His voice came out all scratchy. "S-so did you?"

"What?" she asked.

"You know...eat him?"

"No. Not really. I mean, I did nibble on his nipples a little. But the man was insatiable with the fucking. I mean, he just kept pounding me from behind, and it went on and on and on. Finally, after three orgasms, I passed out."

Andrus blew out a huge breath. "Wow," he croaked, and then cleared his throat. "That s-s-sounds awful."

She shrugged. "It was okay. Not really my thing."

"Nuh-nuh-no?"

Why did Andrus look so flustered?

"My thing is really more in the foreplay department—you know—I like it when the man takes his time and uses his tongue on every inch of my body. Then, I like to use my mouth and bring him right up to the edge a few times before I let him slide it in nice and slow." She sighed. *Damn. That sounded really good right about now.*

Sadie? What the hell? Why are you telling him all this?

She snapped to her senses. "Ohmygod. I can't believe I just said that—are you okay? You're sweating."

He bobbed his head. "Ye-yes. Fine," he said with a scratchy voice.

"Okay. Good. Well, I hope that was helpful." *Because for the life of me, I have no clue why I just told you all that stuff.* Though every word was true. However, it was like she knew what would turn him on and couldn't resist doing it.

"Yep." He turned and marched straight from the room.

"Hey! Where are you going?"

"I need to take care of something," he called from somewhere inside the house.

"Okay! But you and I are going on a training date tonight! So we're having a crash course in wooing starting after lunch!"

He didn't reply, but hopefully he'd heard her.

Damn, that was really weird. Maybe she scared him off with her little too much information?

⤜⤛

Andrus headed straight for his bedroom—on the other side of the house from Sadie—locked the door, got out some lotion, stripped off his shirt, and dropped his jeans.

He'd never felt so hard in his entire life, and this raging erection would not be going away on its own.

What the hell is this woman trying to do to me? he thought as he took his cock in his hand and started stroking, imagining it was the inner sanctum of Sadie's hot, wet body milking him hard.

Images of taking her naked from behind, licking every inch of her body, of her taking his cock in her mouth, pummeled his mind. He imagined cupping her breasts and sucking on her sweet nipples as she moaned in ecstasy.

Godsdammit. So close. So close. He was too high on arousal to try to talk himself down or to rationalize how wanting her was wrong.

Instead, he just imagined the sweet taste of her lips on his mouth while he fucked her hard—now from the front so he could see her face when he slid his large cock in and out of her, over and over again until he finally felt her walls contracting around him, begging for his cum. And then...he'd give it to her and...

"Sadie," he groaned, spilling himself into his tee shirt. "Fuck! Oh gods. Fuck." He kept coming and coming, like it would never end. *Feels so godsdamned good—*

"Andrus?" There was a knock on his door. "You okay?"

Oh hell. He dropped his head, panting hard. "Yeah," he said, in a raspy low voice. "Just doing some push-ups."

"Oh. Okay. I thought I heard you calling my name right before you said, 'Fuck. Oh gods. Fuck.'"

He winced. "No. Just...cut myself shaving." *Sonofabitch. Did I have to be so loud?*

"I just wanted to be sure you heard me? I think it's better if I show you what I like, and then you can do it with me tonight."

Do it? "Sorry?"

"You know, dinner? After I go over what I think works with a woman."

"Uh yeah. Dinner. I'll pick a place."

"Okay. Enjoy your push-ups and shaving."

"Fuck," he whispered, looking down at his cock. She'd just made him hard again.

He sighed and grabbed the bottle of lotion.

❧

That man was totally pleasuring himself to me. What in the world? Honestly, it was kind of sexy. Especially the part about imagining him behind that closed door with his erection in his big hand, that huge bicep flexing and bulging as he pumped.

"Wow." She fanned herself, thinking she might need to take another shower.

Sadie, don't go there. He might be a little attracted to you, but he is going to meet his Mrs. Andrus. It wouldn't be doing herself any favors to entertain thoughts of getting intimate with the man.

No. This is strictly business. Even if her heart said it wasn't.

Later that afternoon, Sadie pulled a reluctant Andrus away from his laptop. Surprisingly, for a man who'd spent a few hours jerking off, he looked tenser than ever.

I wonder if it's an immortal thing. She tried not to judge. And not to let it turn her on again. She seriously came *this* close to rubbing one out herself just to relieve the pressure.

"Okay." She sat him down in the living room, where he took the large white sofa, and she took the overstuffed armchair. "Let's start with a little visualization exercise. Do you know what this woman looks like?"

"I am told her name is Charlotte, and no, I do not," he replied.

That's a lovely name. One of her cousins on her mother's side was named Charlotte though she hadn't seen her since she was little—before her biological mother left.

"Okay. No problem. So you're going to be introduced to Charlotte at a party, right?"

"Correct."

"Good. Now, close your eyes," she instructed.

"Why?"

"Just trust me, it's easier to visualize with your eyes closed."

He grumbled and then reluctantly complied.

"Good. Now, imagine you're in a crowded bar. It's evening and you've put on your nicest suit, combed your hair—"

"Combs are for pansies."

"Uh no, they're not. But okay; you've done that cute thing with your hair that makes it all spikey and messy."

"You think it is...cute?" he asked, sounding insulted. "I am an assassin."

"Whatever. Your hair looks deadly. It screams 'Don't fuck with me.'"

"This is better." With his eyes closed, his dark lashes fanning along the crease of his lids, he smiled with those plump little bad-boy lips.

I swear, his lips were created for buying female forgiveness.

She continued, "You walk into the room, and you see her waiting for you at the bar."

"How will I know it's her?"

"Hmm..." she replied. "How did you plan to meet her at the party?"

"I suppose Cimil will introduce us."

"Fine. Cimil is there and—"

"I punch her in the face?" he said.

"Andrus, come on. I'm trying to help you. Just pretend you don't want to punch Cimil in the face and she introduces the two of you. And before you ask, you don't need to know what the woman looks like, because we're focusing on you. Just see yourself as you approach her."

"I look very handsome," he said seriously. "As usual."

Sadie cracked a smile. "Now I want you to think of two goals when you greet her: One, you want to make her feel relaxed and open to you. Second, you want her to feel safe with you. So what's the first thing you do?"

"I show her my sword."

"What? No. That is not the first thing—or the second or third—a girl wants to see when she meets a guy."

"You really suggest I show her *that*?" He opened his stunning turquoise eyes and smiled devilishly.

It sent her pulse racing. "She doesn't want to see your penis either, Andrus." Although, it certainly was magnificent.

He shrugged. "Her loss."

"Close your eyes." She shot him a look, and he once again obeyed. "Okay. The first thing you want to do is show her your *smile*. Not forced or fake, but a genuine smile that reflects in your eyes. Like the one you just showed me. If you do it right, it will make her heart speed up."

"Did my smile just do that to you?" he asked.

Yes. Absolutely. "Let's focus on you and her, please. Then, I want you to visualize reaching out your hand and introducing yourself. When you take her hand, let her feel the warmth of your skin and squeeze her hand—not too hard, though. Think about how her hand feels in yours, and look into her eyes. Let her know you're there to be with her and no one else. Then make sure she's taken care of—ask what she wants to drink."

"What if she already has one?"

"Then ask her if she'd like to sit somewhere quieter."

"What if all of the tables are taken or there is nowhere quiet to sit?" he asked.

"Then ask how she likes the place or how she's enjoying the party. It doesn't matter. You just want to make sure she knows you're thinking about her comfort without going crazy or coming on too heavy. Guys who try too hard make women feel uncomfortable. And that leads me to your body language: no arm crossing, no standing too close— let her come closer when she's ready. And, whatever you do, do not—and I mean do *not*— stare at her breasts."

"This is no fun."

"Andrus, this isn't about your fun; it's about her. You're playing a character—a different version of yourself that will make her want to get to know you. If you play your cards right, she'll let you actually see her breasts later." The thought of him doing so made her feel a little jealous.

"It sounds like you're trying to teach me how to

seduce a woman."

"Well, I guess in a way I am. If you act like a gentleman and treat a woman well, that can be just as sexy as—"

"Showing her my giant cock?" he said and cracked a big smile.

Maybe. "No. Absolutely not. The point is, when you're with her, you want to be present and aware of her needs. You pull out her chair for her, you make sure the waiter gets her a drink. One of the best techniques they teach actors is the power of eye contact, so if you find yourself unsure of what to say, look in her eyes while you're thinking. You don't snap, look at other women, snarl, tell her to be silent or pay attention to everyone in the room except her."

"Ah. You are referring to my date with Alexis." His turquoise eyes burned with intense curiosity.

"You're supposed to have your eyes closed," she reminded him.

"When I close them, I can only see your face anyway. Might as well have them open."

Her pulse quickened and her stomach fluttered. "Really? I mean. Of course, you're listening to my voice. But yes, I was referring to your date. That was a great example of what not to do. You dismissed her when she spoke and you had your eyes on everything except for her."

"I saw only one woman worth looking at that evening," he said with that deep, deep masculine voice that made her bones vibrate and her heart lunge. What was he trying to do to her? Her body began feeling hot and needy and—*God, he's so sexy. He so doesn't need my help with women.*

"We-well...that's a nice thing to say, considering you tried to kill me." She laughed nervously, desperately trying to change the conversation.

"A minor detail," he said, still staring with that intense gaze.

"Says you. I was terrified."

"I quite enjoyed it. It gave me the opportunity to experience your warm body beneath me."

Her lungs stopped functioning for a brief moment while she tried not to imagine him on top of her. It didn't work. *Oh damn, it's so hot in here.* "I think there are better ways to get a woman into that position. And don't say 'showing her your cock.'"

He laughed. "You're no fun."

"I'm plenty of fun. Can we get back to your date?" *Please, before I explode while sitting here with you?*

"I think I grasped the concept—make her feel like the center of attention, don't overdo it because it will make her uncomfortable, and make her feel relaxed. Is that about it?"

"Well, yeah. That's the basic concept. Let's do some exercises with body lan—"

"Good." He stood from the couch. "I have some work to take care of."

"But I thought we could go over some—"

He held out his hand. "I'm more of a..." his eyes flickered up and down her body, "a hands-on kind of learner. Let us save our energy for tonight."

Sadie's pulse fluttered like mad. Why did it sound like he meant something more? And why did she desperately hope he did? And why did she have the distinct feeling he was going to have some more "me time"?

Wow. Those immortal men certainly have a ravenous libido. Which, of course, only made her want him more. The thought of him having his way with her all night long sounded incredibly hot.

"Okay. We'll continue tonight at dinner. Did you pick a restaurant?" she asked.

"I have. Be ready to eat at eight o'clock." He turned to leave. "Oh, and by the way, Tommaso is coming to keep an eye on you for a few hours today. I need to take care of a few things."

"I can stay by myself," she said.

He smiled, and it was a sexy cocky little smile. *Do his bad-boy lips know any other kind?*

"Yes," he said, "but this would not make you feel safe. And per your instructions, a gentleman always strives to make the lady feel safe." He dipped his head and left the room, leaving her feeling like a warm, gooey pile of sexual need. This man was so different from the Andrus she'd first met, like he'd shed a few tons of ice around his soul. His sexual magnetism was off the charts. As was his charm and raw masculine energy and...

Dammit, why does he have to be taken?

A little after five in the afternoon, the dog Niccolo—a really cute, elderly cocker spaniel she'd learned Andrus had adopted from the local pound—began barking, alerting them that Tommaso was at the front door. When she opened it, the word "wow" came to mind. He looked like he'd just come from a runway shoot, wearing a black suit, deep purple shirt, and black tie.

He bent forward to kiss her cheek. "Well, if it isn't my favorite runaway mortal."

"Hi, Tommaso." She gave him a quick hug. "It if isn't my favorite lady's man." He'd seriously had a line of women and men—asking him to dance, drink, or have sex—when they were at that club. Honestly, the man was gorgeous. Drop-dead frigging insanely gorgeous. But Andrus's rough edges and cavalier attitude made him a little badder, a little sexier, and maybe a little more challenging. *Yeah, I'm definitely on Team Andrus.*

Tommaso straightened his tie and stepped inside. "Well, I am going to be off the market soon, so it's nice to do a little innocent socializing before the big day."

She shut the door behind him. "Are you excited?"

"Nervous, more than anything. I've been in love before, but I'm told it's much more intense with a mate. Some mates are so connected they can hear each other's thoughts, feel each other's emotions. It is rumored that even the great Niccolo DiConti, former vampire general, experiences his mate's PMS once a month."

Funny. The cocker spaniel's name is Niccolo. "Oh. That does sound scary. If my husband knew what went on inside my head when I'm hormonal, I think he'd run for the hills."

Andrus appeared behind him, still wearing his faded, sexy-as-hell button flies, and a thin, light blue sweater that made his eyes sparkle. "Yes, I bet it's quite the dirty place. But some of us men happen to enjoy that."

"Andrus." Tommaso dipped his head.

"Thanks for coming," Andrus said. "And thank you for swearing on your eternal soul that you will not remove her from the house."

"Yeah, sorry about that," Tommaso said.

Andrus shot him a look. "I'll be back in a few hours."

"Did you find a lead?" Tommaso asked.

"In fact, I did. I'll tell you more when I return." He headed for the door.

"Andrus?" she said, unsure of what she wanted to say. "You look nice out of your leather pants." *Wait. That came out wrong.* "I meant, you look hot in jeans." *Wait. That came out wrong, too.* "You don't look as hard anymore." *Oh no. Stop it mouth.* "Never mind."

He gave her an odd look and then flashed a devilish smile. "Like I said, I promised not to judge."

He went out the front door, and she watched him walk away, that hard ass flexing into perfect mounds as he moved. *Goddammit. I'm so in trouble.*

CHAPTER FIFTEEN

He is definitely not a Maaskab, Andrus thought to himself while staring down at the bloated corpse lying across the cold stainless steel autopsy table.

"So, I'm guessing from the seaweed stuck in his hair that the man drowned?" Andrus asked the mortician, who was an older gentleman, likely in his sixties, snacking on a pastrami sandwich, the mayo dripping all over the front of his bloodstained lab coat.

Gods. He did not just wipe that glob and eat it. I am thoroughly revolted. And this coming from a person who'd seen his fair share of repulsive things in his life. Like the time he and his men had tracked down a nest of Obscuros—evil vampires—who ran a nursing home in Caracas. Obviously, they were treating the poor helpless mortals like their personal blood buffet, but from the bodies they found, there was much more going on.

I shall never forget the cold smiles on their wrinkly faces. He shivered.

"Yeah," the mortician said, smacking away on his lunch. "I can't discuss the nature of his death since there needs to be a full autopsy and police investigation, but since you're a friend of Cimil's, I can say we assume he drowned."

Why Cimil had a personal relationship with the county coroner, one could only guess. Perhaps it was the nature of her work or out of convenience. Things tended to end up dead when she was around. And by things, he meant people. Generally bad people, but not always.

Andrus scratched his beard. "Thank you. If you find out anything more, please call me. I'll make it worth your while." He jotted down his number and headed out to his SUV.

Tim was dead, but from the look of him, he'd been dead for several days. That meant Tim had not been the one to attack Sadie at the club last night. And that meant he'd have to continue keeping an eye on her.

Fuck. Now he had no idea what to do. With every passing second, he felt more drawn to her—her voice, her glib little laugh, her defiant nature. And dammit if she didn't make him harder than reinforced steel. Especially seeing her in those tight little jeans that accentuated the curve of her hips. She probably wore one of her lacy little thongs underneath. Oh yes, he'd seen the entire collection when he'd packed up her belongings before going to retrieve her from Tommaso's house last night. Of course, she hadn't been there because she refused to obey his orders, which strangely made him even more fucking hot for her.

Feisty little she-devil takes orders from no one.

Sexually speaking, he'd never felt more potent

chemistry with anyone. Regardless, it would not be fair to start something with her, knowing he was going to meet the second love of his existence within a few days. He'd experienced the mate connection before, and it was all consuming. One might find another person attractive. One might even develop romantic feelings for another, but it paled in comparison to the deep, gnawing insatiable love and passion one felt for a mate. He could promise Sadie the stars and the moon and feel in his heart it wasn't a lie, but the moment he set eyes on his mate, nothing else would matter. Even if this woman rejected him at the mixer because he failed to be chivalrous, he'd spend the rest of his days pursuing her. He wouldn't be able to stop himself.

Great. That sounds like fun.

Tonight, it would be best if he learned what he could from Sadie, because clearly that woman knew something about seduction, given his obsessive thoughts about her. She could help him hit it out of the park with Charlotte and avoid a lifetime of pure agony.

Now, if he could just stop lusting after Sadie, everything would be perfect. *On the other hand, perhaps if you got Sadie out of your system?* She was, after all, a modern woman who seemed extremely comfortable with a little casual fucking. As long as he was forthcoming and honest about their relationship, a little messing around would be fair game.

Yes, tonight, I will work on my wooing technique with Sadie. Perhaps she'll reward me with a little prize.

He only hoped it would be enough if he succeeded.

৵৹৵

Tommaso was totally cheating at cards. How did she know? Because every time he switched out a card, he tried to distract her from his sleight of hand with a little flirtation.

She laid down her cards. "Full house. Read 'em and weep, pretty boy." Her father had taught her and her sister to play cards when they were little. It was the time before iPads, so whenever they took vacations—generally camping or somewhere quiet and away from the crowds her father despised—they played cards. Poker, blackjack, gin rummy, she knew them all. Funny, though, her father always beat them, like he had X-ray vision and always knew their hands.

"I cannot believe you won again." He laid down his cards and threw up his hands. "You're impossible to beat—must be your dress that's distracting me."

She smiled. She'd decided to wear her little black dress, the one with no back coverage and a draping neckline that showed her cleavage. She'd also worn her brown hair up in a loose twist that showed off her long neck and smooth shoulders. Makeup covered the quickly fading marks from the night before.

"Maybe if you stopped cheating and tried to focus on the game, you could win," she replied, looking at her watch. It was almost eight o'clock, but she hadn't seen Andrus yet.

Tommaso flashed a charming smile and dipped his head. "But cheating is so much fun."

She shook her head. "Is it true you used to be evil?" she asked.

"Eh." He shrugged his broad shoulders. "I prefer to say morally challenged. But yes, I lived for many years possessed by evil. I'm all better now. The cheating is just because I find that a little bad behavior takes the edge off. Being good all the time is too much pressure."

"It's kind of weird, but I know what you mean. My dad always pushed me to be perfect in everything—a 'good girl.' I think it just pushed me to do bad things for a little relief, to prove to myself I was still in control." Her father had also been a very antisocial man. Outside of his dentist practice, he saw no one except for their stepmother, her, and her sister. He never allowed anyone to come to the house either. It made her rebellious years more rebellious than usual because she felt even more caged by him. Now, however, he'd loosened up a bit, although he still worried about her more than he should.

"And," Tommaso leaned forward, "do you still enjoy doing bad things?"

"Not anymore. Yes, I cuss and lose my temper sometimes. But bad bad? No. I'm a good girl."

"Oh really?" Tommaso cocked a dark brow. "Then why do I get a hidden naughty-girl vibe from you?"

"Are you flirting with her, Tommaso?" Andrus's deep, deep voice soared through the dining room like a flying hammer on a mission to smash something to bits.

Sadie's heart bounced, and her body shivered at the sight of Andrus, who looked like a tall, delicious piece of sexy man in a tailored dark suit and blue shirt that matched his eyes. His tie was a few shades darker than the shirt and his shoes were actual shoes. Polished black leather.

Her breath stuck in her lungs. "Wow," she gasped. "You look, um..." *fuckable.* "Nice."

He lifted a brow. "Nice?"

"Sorry." She cleared the lust in her throat. "I mean dangerous and deadly." *And so fuckable.* Some large men couldn't pull off a suit—they looked like rhinos trying to fit into the skin of a gazelle—but Andrus looked sleek and tall and...*hmmm*...as delicious as the first time she'd laid eyes on him. "I just hope you don't try to murder me with a steak knife."

He smiled, possibly noting her obvious drooling. "No knives where we're going."

"Oh, I can't wait."

CHAPTER SIXTEEN

"Seriously, Andrus? You said no knives."

"That is not a knife." His eyes washed over the woman in the shiny pink belly-dancing costume, balancing a giant blade on her head while expertly shimmying her coin-covered hips.

No, that certainly wasn't. It was a huge fucking sword. Should she warn the woman not to approach Andrus?

The waiter, dressed in an Aladdin outfit, showed them to their "table"—a giant silver tray with legs, surrounded by a bunch of round pillows. How the hell was she going to sit in her dress?

"Whatever you do, don't look under the table," Sadie said, carefully kneeling down. "And by the way, you get a fail on making me feel special."

"Now I'm definitely going to look under the table. And why did I fail?" he said, mocking a defensive tone.

"You were totally checking out that woman. That's a big no-no on a date."

Andrus removed his coat, laid it over the cushion next to him, and sat down on his pillow across from her. "I was merely looking at her and thinking how she's got nothing on you. Especially in that dress you're wearing. Are you trying to kill me with heatstroke?" He grinned and fanned his face.

"Oh." Sadie tilted her head. "Good save, my man. Good save." She high-fived him from across the table.

He dipped his head and grinned. "Thank you. Thank you very much."

"So what made you pick this place?" she asked. Although it was located in some out-of-the-way strip mall, the interior was pretty cool—full-blown Moroccan style, with dark silky fabric billowing from the ceiling and Persian rugs on the floor. She felt like she'd been transported to a Lawrence of Arabia film.

"I think eating with your hands can be a very sensual experience," he replied, in that deep, masculine sensual voice that made her bones tingle.

Dear Magic Genie of Lust, help me get through this evening in one piece.

Sadie then noticed there were no utensils set out. She loved it. But this wasn't about her tonight. It was about him learning to be aware of his woman.

"And what made you think I would want to eat with my hands?" she asked.

"Ah. Well, two things. You seem to enjoy experiences more than simply completing tasks. For you, it's all about the journey."

"Wow. I'm floored. How'd you know that?" They barely knew each other.

"By the way you carry yourself and speak. There's a hint of hunger or thirst in everything you do. You have the spirit of an adventurer."

Yes, he was dead on, and it was amazing how well he read her.

He added, "That, and I thought you'd feel more comfortable if there weren't any knives on the table." He leaned in. "Of course, that doesn't mean I didn't bring my own."

She laughed. "To make me feel safe?"

"Of course."

"Wow." She gave him a little clap. "I'm impressed, Andrus. You really did think of me."

"Good. Now we can enjoy our meal and relax. What would you like to drink?"

"Ummm...I think I'd like white wine. The food looks kind of spicy."

Just then, the server showed up with a large golden bowl, a tea-kettle-looking thing, and two hand towels.

"Place your hands over the bowl," Andrus instructed.

She stretched out her arms, and Andrus took her hands, gently stroking her palms with his fingertips, as the waiter poured warm floral-scented water. The sensation of his touch shot sensual goose bumps over her skin, also sparking little tingles over her erogenous zones. He felt so good, like he had some delicious current of hot manly sexual goodness surging through his body.

He took the hand towels from the server and slowly rubbed her hands dry, staring into her eyes.

Wow. I think I just had a finger-gasm. He'd touched her hand, but she felt its sexual effects all the way down to her toes.

Once the handwashing was complete, he ordered her a bottle of wine and made a few recommendations on dishes—a very gentlemanly thing to do. She had to admit that seeing Andrus so effortlessly charm his way through dinner made her wonder why the hell he needed her at all.

"Andrus? Can I ask you something?"

"You just did." He smirked.

"Funny boy. Seriously, though, I haven't taught you a thing. Yet here you are with all of the manners of a prince."

He rubbed his whiskered chin. "That's because I come from a very wealthy and prestigious Russian family." He leaned in and whispered, "I was once quite skilled at the art of behaving civilized."

"But Andrus Gray? That doesn't sound Russian."

"My mother, gods rest her soul, was from the Estonia region, her surname Andrus. Grebenshchikov was my father's last name. I changed my last name after I became immortal in order to put a little distance between me and my family." He shrugged. "I never thought about changing it back after they were gone, but I guess I should."

Staring at this man, it began to sink in what it

truly meant to have been alive as long as he had. Three hundred and thirty-two years. She wondered what the world looked like back then and how much he'd seen over what equated to four or five lifetimes. Then again, he'd spent most of it hunting and killing and it didn't sound like he enjoyed it much.

Poor guy. Someday, she'd ask him about it.

"Well," she said, leaning in, "I am very impressed by your three-hundred-year-old manners. You still got it, baby." She winked.

"Thank you." He dipped his head of messy, man-sex-kitten hair. "Perhaps I'm not as rusty as I thought. To be frank, until I met you, I believed that part of me was—"

The waiter showed up with their wine, interrupting their very interesting conversation. She did the honors before the waiter filled their glasses.

The wine was perfect. "Good choice." She lifted her glass to him. "So you were saying?"

"Perhaps this subject is best left for another day. Never is also good."

"No. I want to know, Andrus." She found everything about him fascinating.

He glanced over the table at her, clearly contemplating whether or not to share.

"I promise not to judge," she said, using his own line.

He flashed a warm grin with those sinfully sexy

lips. "Very well. I believed that side of me was dead."

"Because you spent too long killing," she leaned in to whisper, "vampires?"

"Yes and no. My life before I became what I am isn't something I enjoy remembering. I had parents and a sister and we loved each other. Then one day, I met Reyna—my mate and a very cruel woman who used me. I forgot all about who I was and who I loved. I never said goodbye to anyone, and my family died never knowing what happened to me, the worse part being that I didn't care. Then I became enslaved to the gods and the only things I cared about were my men, killing, and getting my freedom back."

Jesus. She couldn't imagine living through that. Her family was her anchor, and being given some sort of mate-whammy to forget the people she loved would be like dying a slow death. At least on a subconscious level because she could never forget them.

"And now? How do you feel about your life as a free man?" she asked.

"I am beginning to see that caring for Matty and Helena were distractions from confronting my pain. Three hundred years of it."

"Who are Helena and Matty?"

He sipped his wine in one gulp. "Helena is the woman I love—or did love—I don't know anymore. But she is mated to the Executioner."

Yikes. "He sounds dreamy."

"That is just his nickname. His real name is Niccolo DiConti. He was Reyna's general. She was the queen of all vampires."

"Holy crap. Really?" *And how strange. He named the dog after this guy.*

"I cared for Niccolo's mate, Helena, while he was away. I was there for the birth of their daughter and treated her as my own."

Oh, wow. "So Matty is the little girl in the photo you had in your duffle bag."

He dipped his head and played with the base of his glass while staring at the pale golden-yellow liquid inside. "Yes. That is Matty. And there is nothing I won't do for her."

"So what happened?" she asked.

"Niccolo walked in on Helena and me hugging in the kitchen. She'd been crying because I told her I was going to leave. With Niccolo home again, there was no reason for me to stay. And with our temperaments, it was only a question of time before we went head to head. So I told her I loved her. And Matty. And that I would always be there for them. But when Niccolo walked in, he assumed the worst—that she and I were embracing as lovers."

"Oh no. I'm guessing that didn't go over so well." *And that explains the dog's name.*

"No. Helena stepped in between us and told me to back off, that she'd explain to Niccolo, but then he said those magic words, and I couldn't help myself. I swung over Helena's head and knocked him across the room."

"What did he say to set you off?"

"That a woman as good as Helena would never love a dishonorable man like me."

Sadie reached out and touched his hand with the tip of her finger. "I'm so sorry, Andrus. That couldn't have been easy."

"I didn't want it to end like that. I thought if I left before things got bad, I could still come back and visit every once in a while. Now, I will never be welcome in their home again."

"Things could change, Andrus."

"That is the downside about being immortal. The world changes, we do not—at least, not in a good way. The years embitter us, make us more stubborn and less forgiving. I looked after that man's wife and child, and I behaved with honor. Yet, instead of thanking me, he accused me of trying to take his place. How does someone forgive that?"

Sadie shrugged. "You're right. You should definitely shank him."

Andrus cracked a smile. "Shank?

"You know, prison style? With a homemade blade made from a toothbrush or spoon. Go gangsta on the man."

Andrus chuckled before a pensive expression washed over him. "Sadly, that asshole is Matty's father. It would be very dishonorable to murder him. But now I realize that maybe I didn't love Helena so much as I loved feeling like part of a family again and having someone to protect. I think it's simply in my nature."

It was just too sweet. And sentimental and...hotter than hell. "Well, the only thing you can do now is hope Niccolo comes to his senses and for you to move on with your life."

Andrus flashed a hard look at Sadie as if she'd hit a nerve. "Unfortunately, Cimil has prophesized that I am to father a son and that son will grow up to be Matty's mate. My life will forever be intertwined with theirs."

Sadie gasped. "Oh." That put an entirely different spin on things.

"But if it means Matty's happiness, I have little choice. This is why I must meet this Charlotte and win her over—Cimil says for some reason she will not be so open to be mated to me."

Sadie felt a twinge of jealousy. Whoever this woman was, she'd be a goddamned idiot if she didn't fall head over heels for Andrus. Sure, he had his rough edges, but the man had a sweet streak and was so goddamned good looking that he could have just about any woman in the world.

"So if you blow it," Sadie sighed, "you blow it for Matty."

"Exactly."

She'd sort of hoped that this mate thing wasn't

such a done deal, but now this settled it. She couldn't like Andrus. Not even a little. "Well, if you could make me want you, I'm sure you'll have no problem getting her to warm up to you."

Crap. Did I just say that? Her head snapped up to meet Andrus's intensely carnal gaze burning from across the table.

Her breath stuck in her throat. That look triggered something deep inside her, something she'd never known existed. It was like an ache or a thirst that made her insides feel like they were on fire and he was the only thing capable of providing relief. Suddenly, she found herself wanting him so badly it hurt. Could he tell? Could he see it in her eyes?

"Sadie," he said, his voice low and gruff, "I want to ask you something. Something I have no right asking, but I must. I'd like to have—"

Just then the loud clanking of cymbals and a highly coordinated giggling belly shimmied up to Andrus's ear. *Oh, no. The scarf. He got scarved!*

Andrus's turquoise gaze slowly peeled away from Sadie, and he glared up at the smiling belly dancer.

"I'm afraid you've been summoned, Andrus." Sadie had really, really wanted to hear what Andrus was about to say, but the distraction couldn't have come at a better time.

She couldn't want him. She couldn't be thinking of doing what she'd obviously been thinking of doing. *You can't, Sadie. This guy isn't for you. He's going to break your heart.*

Andrus shot Sadie a look.

"What, are you afraid?" she egged him on.

He grumbled something, but she couldn't hear it over the music and rhythmic clanking.

With the grace of a gazelle, Andrus pulled his large, muscled frame up off the floor and stood, towering over the petite, curvy woman with loads of eyeliner and a green veil.

She led him away from the table toward the center of the room where everyone could see.

Oh, the horror. He looks like he's going to strangle the woman.

Facing Andrus, the woman urged him to follow along by placing her hands on his hips while the other patrons began clapping. Andrus stood there, no hip action whatsoever as he watched the woman dancing in front of him encouragingly.

He glanced over at Sadie with a scowl.

"Oh, come on, Andrus. Give us a little dance." Sadie placed her palms together in the prayer position. "Pleeease?"

Andrus's large chest expanded with a breath, and then he held up his index finger and walked over to the corner of the room where the woman's sword rested against the wall.

Oh no. What's he going to do with that?

He returned to the woman. "I'm afraid this is the only dance I know besides a waltz."

He turned away from her and balanced the edge of the sword on his head. Then he carefully squatted with a straight back and folded his arms over his chest. Holding his torso almost completely still, keeping the knife balanced, he began kicking his legs, doing that Russian dance—she didn't know the name. The crowd and belly dancer clapped along as he threw out his arms and kicked while keeping that sword steady. Then he stood, placed the sword between his teeth and bent down into a handstand. He walked across the open spot of the floor and then swung his legs over his head and landed on his feet.

Sadie realized her mouth had been hanging wide open the entire time. Seeing Andrus, this huge tank of muscles, laughing and doing some crazy Russian kick squat dance was downright hysterical.

Everyone clapped as Andrus took a bow and then returned the sword to the dancer.

He strutted back to the table, thoroughly enjoying the attention from every woman in the room. He truly was a hot man.

Grinning from ear to ear, he sat across from Sadie, gloating.

"Show off." She laughed.

"It was either that or show you my uncoordinated hip rolls. I did not want you to feel uncomfortable."

She lifted a brow. "Really? You strike me as a

man who knows lots of hip moves, but maybe those are more of the back and forth kind—not the side to side."

"You assume correctly." His smile melted away into a lusty gaze that sizzled from across the table. "I'm happy to show you, if you like," he said in a deep, sensual bedroom voice.

She wanted to say no and that it was not a good idea. He was practically spoken for, and she was beginning to fall in serious like. But then, if in a few days' time he'd be off the market, did she really want to pass up the chance? After all, the man was perfection in the physical department and there was no denying now that she may be interested to see how that hip action coordinated with the rest of his hard, chiseled body. Then there was all of the other stuff about him she was beginning to more than just like—his fearlessness, the way he tried to hide his soft underbelly, his sense of loyalty.

God, I so fucking want him.

She was about to speak when he began laughing.

"Dear gods, woman, don't look so horrified. It was merely a joke."

She gulped. "Oh. Yeah. Of course." Her voice had come out all shaky, so she took her glass of wine and threw it back. "But that's too bad because I would've said yes."

His laughter crashed and burned and several long moments of silence passed before he spoke.

"You realize that there can't be anything between us. I'll meet Charlotte and want no other."

"Yeah, I know," Sadie said.

"And you don't care?"

She made a little shrug. "I wouldn't say that. But how can I resist having you for a night after you showed me that dance move?" She winked.

"Check!" he yelled for the waiter.

⚭

Cimil sat at her desk, pulling on the roots of her red hair plus one gray. "This can't be right. It just can't be." She was hearing and seeing so many strange things from the dead, none of it making any sense.

It seemed that being banished and having her powers removed was a bigger obstacle than she'd anticipated. She could still commune with the dead, as that was more of a skill than a power, but she could no longer get inside their heads, which was how she pieced together events from the future. The pool of souls, where the dead hung out until they decided if they wanted to come back for another spin in a people suit or move on to rejoin the cosmic soup of energy, existed in a place beyond the confines of time. But the dead were practically useless to her if she wasn't able to sift through their Mount Fuji-sized pile of memories with a mere blink of an eye. And without her ability to bend the Universe to her will—okay, it was really more of a nudge—she could no longer persuade or change the outcome of events. Things were now taking on courses of their own. *Completely random, unpredictable chaos. As opposed to my awesome predictable chaos with an evil cherry on top. This is not good.*

If she didn't find some way to intercede, everything would begin falling apart—Zac would go bonkers, the world would probably end up back on a collision course to the apocalypse again. *And dammit!* They'd just gone through this. It had been so close, ninety percent of the sea turtle population had abandoned ship and returned to their planet.

Without even offering to take me along. Damned sea turtles.

Cimil's cell phone began playing "You're the Best" from the *Karate Kid* soundtrack. "Yo, baby. Wassup?"

"Gah-rarar-garrr-kah-kah-rarrr..."

"Really?" Cimil pinched her brow. "Godsdammit. Can't a quasi-evil goddess ever catch a break?"

"Rarrr..."

"I know, right?" She chuckled. *Those Maaskab. Such a riot with their dark humor.* "Okay. Just keep an eye on the woman Sadie. I'm going to have to go over there and stop them."

"Gah," he replied.

"Yep. Catch you later. You're still on for Sunday, yes?"

"Rarrr. Kak. Rarrr...Bleh."

"Excellent. The kids love it when you babysit. Oh. And they asked you to bring some actual cash this time. Playing poker for human thumbs is getting old now that they're past the sucking phase. Thanks, babe."

She ended the call, shaking her head over the news she'd just received from the Maaskab. *How am I going to fix this?*

And she'd never be able to get anything done if she had to rely on actually talking to people and reasoning with them instead of using her powers. And depending solely on her network of immortals and immortal-friendly humans to keep tabs on everything was extremely inefficient when one was trying to manage a few million variables at once.

I need powers. Even if I must steal them from another immortal. Hmmm...maybe she could barter with that Maaskab. At the moment, he was so desperate to find a gal, he'd agree to almost anything. *Even babysitting my evil children.*

For the moment, however, she needed to stop Andrus from making a huge mistake.

She glanced at her watch. "I hope I get there in time."

CHAPTER SEVENTEEN

Sadie hardly spoke a word to Andrus during the drive back to the safe house, but the atmosphere in the SUV was tense. Sexually tense. Then they'd passed the security gate, parked, and practically ran to the front door. The moment they got inside, Andrus slammed the door shut, locked it, and stared at her with a hungry gaze.

God, she was already wet for him. The anticipation had been more arousing than any foreplay ever. She just wanted him to take her. Hard. Right there on the floor.

"What's the matter?" she said, waiting for him to kiss her or touch her or do something.

"I'm remembering what you said about liking it when a man takes his time with you."

"Oh that." She chuckled nervously. "I was just kidding around."

He shook his head from side to side. "Yes, but if it is going to be one time, I want to savor the experience."

What? No! No.

"Sure." She shrugged, trying to play it cool.

He stepped forward with a feral look in his eyes. "I think I'm going to lick you from head to toe.

Then, after I make you come two or three times, I'll fuck you hard and sweet."

Gazing straight up into his turquoise eyes, she stuttered, "Ha-ha-hard and swe-sweet?"

His lips curled up on one side, forming a wicked little smile. "Oh, yes. Two or three times. Immortal style."

"Uh. Okay. That's sounds nice," she said in a faint voice, trying to breathe. "Or..."

"Or?" He reached for her waist and pulled her body against him, his heat, hardness, and smell enveloping her senses in a blanket of gripping lust and need.

"Or," she said, reaching up to slide his jacket off his broad shoulders while keeping her eyes locked onto his. "You could reverse the order."

"Mmmm...I like that idea." He bent his head to hers and the flurry of sparks and kisses and touching went off like a bomb.

His lips and tongue were on her mouth and neck and back again while his hands went to work pulling down the shoulders of her dress, leaving her in just her black strapless bra and lace thong. He stopped only for a moment to appreciate the view, but his little sexy growl indicated he was pleased by what he saw.

Meanwhile, her hands just weren't moving fast enough. She slid off his tie and tore open his shirt, sending buttons flying and giving her access to those hard pecs, rippling abs, and smooth light olive skin. She gripped his shirt by the collar, peeled it down, and allowed her fingertips to soak in the sexy terrain of his masculinity; meanwhile their tongues slid, their mouths sucked, their teeth scraped.

The moment she went for his belt, he scooped her into his arms and carried her to her bedroom. He threw her onto the bed, and she giggled with a bounce.

Andrus stood at the foot of the bed, that fierce, hungry look in his eyes burning through her as he undid his belt and tossed it to the floor. Slowly, he unbuttoned his pants and lowered the zipper.

When his pants fell to the floor, she gasped. Andrus stood entirely naked in front of her, his massive, thick erection jutting out.

"Holy shit," she said. "That thing really is huge."

He shrugged proudly.

"Come here." She motioned with her index finger.

He got on the bed and began crawling towards her. He then reached for her thong and slid it down, his eyes glued between her legs.

"Let me see you," he demanded.

She opened her thighs, watching the expression on his face as he stared at her most intimate spot. Just having his eyes on her pushed her so close that one little touch would set her off.

He reached his hand between her legs, careful not to touch her throbbing bud. Instead, he gently brushed his fingers over her folds and then circled her entrance. Panting hard, she threw back her head, her body screaming for him to be inside her. "Oh God."

"Do you not mean, 'oh demigod'?" Andrus slid his finger inside her, groaning as he found her wet and ready. He slid another in and then pressed his thumb on her c-spot.

She felt her body cave to the need and let go, releasing the euphoric tension. She moaned and tossed and turned her head as he massaged and pushed and withdrew every sinful pulse of pleasure from her core, spurring repeated contractions with tiny flicks of his soft, wet tongue over her bud.

After what felt like ten minutes of solid orgasmic pleasure that left her speechless and breathless, she reopened her eyes and gazed at a smugly triumphant Andrus.

"That was only one orgasm. I have five more to deliver," he said.

Okee dokee! "Do you really think you can?" she said coyly. Of course a man like him could, but challenging him seemed like the optimal way to get him to try just a little bit harder.

"Oh yeah. I most certainly can." He looked down at his twitching erection and gripped it just below the head.

Her entire portfolio of sexual images could not compete with this.

In a deep, slow, gravelly voice, he said, "I'm

going to fuck you so hard that every part of your body will taste my cum."

Oh, yeah. He must be reading my mind. Except that…

"Wait," she said. "Did you bring a condom?"

He flashed the classic "deer in headlights" expression. "No. Did you?"

"No."

"Well, why the hell not? You're the female."

What the…? "Meaning?"

"It's your responsibility to care for your body."

Oh my gods! Really? "So you have zero responsibility in the matter?" she fumed.

"I am a male. We are genetically predisposed to spread our seed to as many females as possible—not that I have, but it does cement the roles and responsibilities question."

She wanted to kill him. Kill. Him. "Andrus, while I completely get that you are from another time, you also weren't born under a rock. It takes two to tango, and the last time I checked, we are both adults."

"Yes, you being the one with the…" he flicked his hand in the direction of her womb, "with the field. While I come equipped with the plow."

"What the hell does that mean?" she seethed.

"It means that if I were a farmer, I'd carry a shotgun and gun down anyone who tried to sow my field without my permission."

She blew out an angry breath. "Get out."

"What?"

"Get. Out."

"Are you saying you should not care for your field?" he asked.

"I'm saying....get out!" she screamed at the top of her lungs, covering her naked body with a sheet.

"Fine. I will."

"Fine!" She watched him gather his pants and head for the door, that muscular, smooth bare ass taunting her as he left.

"What the fuck!" Andrus said, stopping in the doorway, his palms flat against something invisible. "Godsdammit. Minky, have you been here the entire time?"

Who the hell was Andrus talking to? There was no one there.

"Where's Cimil?" he added.

"You rang, baby?" A redheaded woman pushed her way past Andrus inside the room and looked right at Sadie sitting up on the bed, wrapped in a sheet. "Please dear lords of all things holy and garage-sale related, tell me you did not sleep together."

Bob looks so different as a woman.

"No, but what business is it of yours?" Sadie asked, before remembering she was speaking to a real live deity.

"Yes, Cimil," Andrus said, holding his pants over his groin. "What business is it of yours?"

Cimil, who wore black leather shorts and a white

tank with a man's six-pack printed on it, shook her head with frustration, squeezing shut her bright turquoise eyes. "Gods, what did I do to so deserve this from the Universe?"

"Cimiiil?" Andrus growled.

She threw down her hands. "You can't be with her, Andrus. This isn't a trick from the old Cimil fun factory of evil delights, okay?" She then pointed right at Sadie. "And you, young lady, cannot fall in love with him. He is not your destiny."

Sadie slid from the bed, holding the sheet around her body. "I'm sorry. I get that you are a very ancient and divine creature, but nobody tells me who to fall in love with."

"I do!" Cimil barked. "I do. Because Zac and I are stuck in the mortal world until we've paid our dues! And we need every mate-match we can get before Zac goes psycho. Also, it is the Universe's will to have you love another, Sadie."

The part about their paying dues made no sense, just like her statement regarding who she was supposed to love.

"Love another? Like who?" Sadie asked. "Another loser like Tim, who'll attack me and make me forget? Or that other guy who stalked me for two months until he disappeared? Andrus is the only man I've ever met worth loving, so don't tell me what I'm allowed to do."

Cimil shrugged. "We can't all have happy endings. But Andrus is destined to have his. With another woman. And you, little Sippy, cannot get in his way."

"She doesn't even want him. How does that make any sense?" Sadie argued.

"Cimil," Andrus stepped in, "leave us for a moment."

It then dawned on Sadie what she'd just been saying. *Oh my God. I am falling in love with him.*

Cimil huffed. "Fine!" She threw up her hands. "Don't listen to the goddess who's been in existence for seventy thousand years and has single-handedly brought the world to the brink of extinction and back more times than she can remember. Wait. That didn't sound right. What I meant was—"

"Out!" Andrus barked.

Cimil turned and stomped out of the room, closing the door behind her. "Asshole."

"I heard that!" Andrus barked.

"Good!" Cimil yelled back.

Andrus looked at Sadie. He didn't at all seem to mind or notice the fact his bare ass was hanging out. Of course, this was the man who'd proudly showed her his junk the second time they'd met.

"Did you mean what you said?" he asked.

Sadie sat on the edge of the bed facing him. "I don't know."

He sat next to her, still holding his wadded pants to his groin. "I like you very much, too."

Her heart melted. "You do?"

He turned his head and looked down at her with his shimmering turquoise eyes. "Yes. Which is why I am going to leave before this goes any farther. I was kidding myself thinking we could have sex and it not mean anything. And I find myself wanting you more and more with every second that passes."

"At least you'll get over it once you meet Mrs. Wonderful," Sadie pointed out.

"Perhaps. But right now, the only thing I'm thinking about is you and that you do not deserve to be hurt. Falling in love with someone who is taken is torture."

"I just don't understand how a free man isn't free to decide who he wants to be with."

"Maybe you have a point...Maybe I should not go," Andrus mumbled, as if thinking aloud.

"You mean, not go to meet her?" Sadie asked.

He glanced at her with a nod.

But that wouldn't work. If that woman was somewhere out there, who was to say that Andrus wouldn't bump into her two years from now? Ten years from now?

"I don't want to give you my heart, Andrus, and then get tossed aside one day because you meet this woman some other way. I mean, what if we had children and were married. That would break my heart."

"You wish to marry me? And have children?" he asked, completely astonished.

She shrugged pathetically. "I want them with the man I fall in love with. So why wouldn't I want them with you if we were in love?" She looked into his eyes, where little wells of tears had formed. "Are you...crying?"

"No. Men like me do not cry," he said defensively and stood.

"Where are you going?"

"You're right. You're absolutely right." He looked devastated. "This home has been leased for one full year. I would have purchased it for you, but I suspected you would not enjoy living amongst a community of paranoid elitists. I much more imagined you living in a house near the beach or where the atmosphere is lively and youthful—like you."

He'd rented this place for her for an entire year? "So you're going?"

"It is for the best. For both of us," he said.

Her heart sank. "I don't want you to go."

"What other option is there? As you pointed out, there is no path forward for us when *she* will always be out there. And if I stay, I'm merely prolonging the inevitable."

"I guess..." This was hard for her to say. "I'd hoped that you'd meet her and still choose me, as crazy as that sounds."

The look on his face matched the heartbreak she felt inside. "If only such a thing were possible."

She blew out a breath and then smiled at him.

"Don't feel bad. At least we're ending it before anything really happened. It's better to be left wondering what might've been than to find something special and have to give it up because of some cosmic arranged marriage."

"That's absolutely right!" Cimil screamed from the other room.

Andrus shook his head. "I will leave you now."

"Wait. No. I can't stay here," Sadie said.

"Of course you can. I rented the home so you'd be safer."

"I can't take your charity, Andrus. And I will be just fine at my apartment."

"Just because Tim is dead doesn't mean you are safe. The attack at the bar happened after he drowned."

"What? Did you just say that Tim is...dead?"

"Oh." He suddenly looked guilty. "Did I forget to mention that?"

"Uh. Yeah. When did you find this out?"

"Earlier today."

"And you didn't think to tell me?" she asked, feeling thoroughly peeved.

"Well, I..."

"What? You what?" she prodded.

"I saw you in that dress and thought it could wait."

"You're telling me you forgot because you were too busy thinking about getting into my pants?"

"No. Absolutely not—all right. Perhaps, yes."

"Andrus, how could you?"

"Well, I didn't think you cared about him. So what harm would there be in waiting to tell you?"

"The harm is that you knew my creepy ex-boyfriend is dead—poor guy—and that there's something else out there attacking me."

"Which is why you must stay here until the person is found. I will ask Cimil to call in one of her Uchben."

"What the hell is an Uchben?" she asked.

"They are badass immortal soldiers who actually listen to what they are told, unlike some other people I know!" Cimil screamed from the other room. "And Brutus is already on his way. He'll be here in five minutes."

Andrus nodded his head with a stoic expression. "Ah. It seems everything is already settled, then." He dipped his head. "Goodbye, Sadie. It has been a pleasure."

He turned and walked from the room, his bare ass now looking like a target for kicking. She didn't know whether to laugh or cry or scream.

In the space of ten minutes, he'd made her experience every emotion under the sun, including anger because he'd withheld some pretty serious news. But all of that paled in comparison to the fact that he'd just said goodbye.

∽—∼

Andrus had never experienced such a roller coaster of emotions in his entire life. In the space of a few minutes, Sadie had made his heart soar, while the situation managed to crush it. She'd actually wanted him. Wanted him. Not just for sex, but because she thought he was the sort of man she could love and have a life with. It was the first time in his three hundred years any woman had felt that way about him.

During his human years, they wanted him for his money or title. His mate had loved him, but loved herself more and betrayed him. Helena had never thought of him as more than just extended family. But Sadie had real feelings for him all on her own without any cosmic intervention. And the thought of hurting her made him realize that he shared those feelings.

However, the moment she pointed out that she'd hoped he might choose her over his mate, he knew what he had to do: cut ties. It would be cruel of him to allow her to hope for the impossible. He knew damned well how painful it felt to wish for things to be different when they couldn't be. Loving Helena had taught him that lesson.

Yes, Sadie's words had been like a hard slap across his face in a moment when he'd felt blinded by his emotions and desire for Sadie. If he truly cared, he would let her go and hope that Cimil was right: Sadie was destined to love another. He wanted that for her. He wanted her to be happy.

As he packed up his duffle bag, he took a look at Matty's photo. That fangy little grin on her face always warmed his cold heart. It was also yet another reminder of why he could not be with Sadie.

"It seems our destinies have already been decided for us all."

CHAPTER EIGHTEEN

It had been three entire days since Andrus left, and Sadie felt worse with every passing minute. She didn't want to stay in the house, she wanted to move on with her life and try to put it all behind her.

Unfortunately, Cimil had called and told her that there were no leads on this creature, which made her think: What if they never found this monster? She wasn't going to stay in this big house forever or give up the right to live her life—no matter how short that might be.

On the other hand, she wasn't so stupid that she'd ignore the threat. *Time to retreat and regroup.* She would head home to Cleveland for a few weeks and figure out what to do from there.

As for her apartment, she'd learned that Andrus had taken the liberty of paying her back rent so she wouldn't owe the landlord, but that he'd also arranged to have her things moved into storage in a few days. Yeah, he'd planned to move her out of her apartment without her permission. She didn't know whether to be pissed or grateful. It was such an Andrus sort of thing to do. That man's heart was in the right spot, but his way of forcing his charity on her was so...archaic. And sweet. In the end, she'd decided to laugh. What else could she do? Her apartment issue was the least of her concerns. There was some weird creature feeding off her, and the man she'd fallen in love with—completely by surprise—was going to meet his soul mate tonight. Another reason to leave L.A. Ironic, because she finally had the money to stay.

That was the other thing Cimil had explained. She'd chosen Sadie because she'd foreseen in some weird vision about her helping Andrus get back in touch with his human side, which she'd done successfully. Of course, Sadie refused the one hundred thousand dollars that Cimil (Bob) had promised since the beginning because it didn't feel right taking it—she was happy to have been able to help Andrus—but Cimil didn't "take orders from pesky humans."

Sadie still didn't know what to think about all that—the gods, demigods, vampires and these Uchben, this Brutus guy in particular. The man was just as big as Andrus, but his vibe was scary as hell, like he ate bullets for breakfast and perhaps enjoyed dining on small animals he strangled with his own two hands.

He also didn't speak much. Except to the dog Niccolo, who he seemed to have bonded with because the arthritic little fur ball followed him everywhere.

Anyway, she didn't know what she'd do next, but it was time to go home to see her family and try not to focus on the fact that every passing minute brought Andrus closer to meeting his special someone.

I need to get the hell away from here.

She'd swing by her place, grab a few personal things—some photos of her family and the materials from all of her acting classes—and then head out to the airport.

She looked at her watch. Seven o'clock. Less than an hour to party time.

She dug her cell from her purse and dialed Andrus, who answered almost immediately.

"Sadie, are you okay?" His deep voice sent a wave of hollowness through her heart.

"Yeah." She swallowed back her tears. "I'm fine. I just..." *wanted to hear your voice one last time before your heart gets stolen by that woman.* "I wanted to wish you luck tonight. Just remember to make her feel special." *Like you did for me.*

There was a long moment of silence. "Thank you, Sadie. I wish you the same. Whoever this man is in your future, he will be very lucky."

"Thanks," she said quietly. "Take care." Biting back her tears, she ended the call, grabbed her purse, and snuck out of the house before Brutus returned from walking Niccolo.

Andrus had endlessly debated with himself about

whether or not to forget the stupid party. However, each time he thought it through, he landed on the same spot: He had to meet Charlotte. Hell, if he was lucky, meeting this woman might actually make him forget his feelings for Sadie, which were currently eating away at him like battery acid in his heart.

He took one final look at himself in the mirror and gave his messy hair a little fluff with his fingers. *Yeah, you look like the badass that you are.* Spiky hair, his leather pants—the ones with his lucky bloodstains—a plain black tee shirt, and his long leather duster to conceal his sword behind his back.

If this woman was going to be his mate, he wanted her to see the real him. He was tough, deadly, and enjoyed protecting people. There was nothing to be ashamed of because that was who he was now. His human side, the side he'd felt coming alive with Sadie, had been put down almost three hundred years ago for a reason, and trying to resurrect it was stupid. And pointless. *Never again.*

An hour later—*godsdamned traffic!*—Andrus pulled up to the Beverly Hills Hotel. It was a bit cruel that Cimil had booked the party at the same place where he had begun his journey. *To meeting a sexy little she-devil.*

Sitting in his car, he smiled, remembering the look on Sadie's face when he'd opened the hotel suite's door with his pants unzipped. He remembered thinking how sweet she smelled and how beautiful her eyes were—a golden brown that could warm even the coldest of hearts. They had certainly warmed his. Every godsdamned time she looked at him. And that little curvy body... It aroused him just thinking of how she'd looked writhing against the bed, moaning his name. He could still taste her on his tongue. Regrettably, he'd never gotten the chance to sample the rest of her body—those pink little nipples, the base of her back, that little spot behind her knees. Why hadn't he brought a condom? Not that one time would've been enough.

Okay, a box of condoms.

Stop torturing yourself. Be a man, go in there, and meet Charlotte.

He blew out a breath and, with a heavy heart, exited his SUV, handing the keys over to the valet. He made his way through the lobby to the ballroom, where a petite blonde woman with big blue eyes, wearing a flowery dress, sat just out front. Her name tag read "Tula."

"Well, good evening there, sir. May I get your name?" she asked.

"Andrus."

Her eyes widened, and then she grabbed a walkie-talkie sitting on the table. "The eagle has landed. I repeat, the eagle has landed."

He shot her a look, and she shrugged. "Cimil asked me to say that when you arrived."

"Can you tell me where I might find Charlotte?"

"Cimil said she'd come and personally introduce—"

"I will introduce myself. If you'd please simply point her out."

"Yes, sir," Tula said nervously, standing from her chair and pointing to the bar inside. "She's the woman in the green dress with the brown bob."

"Thank you." He dipped his head and made his way into the crowd, who buzzed with laughter and loud conversation over the techno music. As his eyes swept the room, he spotted many familiar faces—a few gods, some vampires who reported to Niccolo DiConti, and several Uchben he'd met over the years. On the far side of the room, the Goddess of—*damn, I can't remember what she's the goddess of*—DJed with her long blonde hair wrapped up in Princess Leia spirals. Belch, the God of Wine and Intoxication, stood behind the bar in his tightie whities, slinging drinks. *That deity really needs some wardrobe help.*

As he walked toward the brunette, who had her back to him and was speaking with Zac, the God of Temptation, he felt his feet stick to the floor. She was right there, less than ten feet away, but his heart didn't want to take another step. He felt it clawing and scratching inside his chest, trying to escape a terrible fate.

How fucked up is this? Finding a mate was the one thing most immortals dreamed of—their special someone who'd love them unconditionally for eternity, who'd be their ideal in bed, who'd place their lives on the line merely to make them happy. Each and every immortal in the ballroom was looking for that kind of love. Yet, here he was dreading it. Hell, he should feel lucky. No one ever got a second mate. Of course, the Universe had considerably fucked him over with the first one, so he supposed the do-over made sense.

Zac looked at him, over the woman's head. "Andrus! There you are!"

The woman turned around and Andrus felt like he'd been kicked in the balls.

Holy fuck. She looks like...Sadie. The auburn hair, the golden-brown eyes, the pouty little lips. They could be sisters.

He could barely breathe, but he managed to shuffle his feet to her.

"Charlotte, may I introduce Andrus," Zac said. "Andrus, Charlotte."

"But you look like...you..." His brain tried to make sense of it.

Charlotte flashed a little smile. "Like Sadie? Yeah, Cimil mentioned that. Sadie's my cousin."

"She never mentioned you," he said.

Charlotte shrugged. "Well, we haven't seen each other since we were little."

Andrus simply stared, his mind whirling a million miles per second. *What the fuck? Is this some sick joke?*

"I'll leave you two lovebirds alone," Zac said.

She went on, "Sadie's mom and my mom haven't spoken in over twenty years. She probably doesn't even remember me."

"How did you end up here at this party?" he asked.

"A couple of weeks ago that crazy redhead found me. Said I needed to meet you. Hey, you look a little...pale. You okay?"

He bobbed his head. "No. Not really."

"It's not a heart attack, is it? Because that weird lady told me you're way older than you look."

"No. Not a heart attack."

"Good." She sipped her fruity-looking cocktail. "Because I don't know CPR."

Andrus tried to breathe, but his chest continued constricting as if a snake had wrapped around his heart. Was his interest in Sadie purely some sort of misdirected affection intended for this woman?

No. I feel...I feel. His head snapped up as he stared into her warm brown eyes. "I feel a connection with you, Charlotte. Like I've known you my entire existence."

"Yeah." She sipped away. "I feel it, too. Like a love at first sight kind of thing. Yanno?"

He shook his head from side to side. "That's the problem. I feel connected with you, but my heart still wants Sadie."

Charlotte's jaw dropped. "But I came here because that crazy redhead promised I'd find my Prince Charming."

He shrugged. "I am sure you and I could make a life together, but you'd never own my heart."

"What? You're rejecting me?"

"I am very sorry to be so blunt and rude, but yes. I am."

"And who the hell are you to reject me? You're nothing but some guy who looks like a hot model in leather pants, but is just some washed-up unemployed foreigner—uh-huh, the redhead told me that you lost your job, but I came anyway. Super mistake." Her hand waved over the front of his body. "You're a big loser."

"Andrus?" he heard a familiar feminine voice behind him. "Please slap that woman."

When he turned, he found a set of big blue eyes staring up at him.

"Who's the bitch?" said Charlotte.

Andrus cleared his throat. "Charlotte, this is Helena, the official leader of the vampire army. Helena, Charlotte."

Helena's blue eyes turned to charcoal black. "Did you just call me a bitch?" she growled.

"Well," Charlotte said, "I didn't...didn't know that—did you say 'vampire'?"

"Helena," Andrus interrupted, "what are you doing here?"

Helena parked her fists on her hips. "I brought

Matty to see you, and Niccolo wanted to speak with you. He feels really bad about the way things ended."

Andrus blinked at her. "Matty is here? And Niccolo wants to apologize?"

"Yeah, they're back at the beach house," Helena replied, keeping a death grip on Charlotte with her eyes. "I also came because I wanted to make sure you didn't fuck things up with your mate." She flashed a glance at Andrus. "Is this really her?"

He bobbed his head. "According to Cimil."

"I think I want to rip out her throat," Helena growled.

Charlotte stepped back. "I didn't mean any disrespect. I had no idea you were a crazy person."

Helena narrowed her eyes. "First you call me a bitch, and now you're calling me crazy?"

"No!" Charlotte looked terrified.

"Good," Helena replied, "because I'd hate to have to slaughter the mother of my future son-in-law."

Charlotte's eyes went wide. "What are you talking about?"

Helena stepped in closer. "Didn't Cimil tell you? You're going to have a baby with Andrus and make my little girl happy someday."

"No," Charlotte replied, "I don't want to be a mother. Especially not with him. You people are crazy." She tried to run around Andrus and Helena, but ended up crashing straight into Cimil.

"Where do ya think you're goin'?" Cimil said with an evil smirk.

"You're all mad. Get away from me!" Charlotte dashed around Cimil and ran out the door.

Andrus gave Cimil a look. "You forgot to tell her what we are?"

Cimil's mouth twisted into a guilty frown. "Whoopsies?"

"Well," Andrus said, "it doesn't matter. I don't want a life with her."

"Damn," Helena said, "I really don't blame you." She rubbed the back of her neck and blew out a breath. "What are we going to do now? Poor Matty."

Andrus looked at Cimil, who was busy staring at the ceiling like a cat watching an invisible game of Ping-Pong. "Cimil, is there any possibility that you were wrong about Charlotte?"

Cimil's head continued moving side to side. "Nope. You felt the connection; she's the one, and you have exactly twenty seconds left until the window closes with her."

Andrus did feel something for the woman, but it was more like a dull ache in his gut, pulling him toward her.

"Andrus?" Helena said with a sorrow-filled voice. "I lied when I said I didn't love you. I do. You're my best friend and brother and protector and Matty's uncle and—I couldn't live with myself if you were unhappy for eternity, which you absolutely would be with that horrible shrew. We'll just have to pray that Matty finds love some other way."

Why did this feel too easy? On the other hand, wasn't it about time for the Universe to cut him a little immortal slack?

"Do you think Matty'll hate me when she grows up?" he asked.

Helena's eyes filled with tears. "She loves you. I think she'll understand."

"I have to go now and find Sadie." *I just hope it's not too late.*

"We'll be at our beach house in Malibu. Come by tomorrow for dinner?" Helena asked.

They had homes all over the world—it was a vampire thing. "I will let you know!" he said, running for the door.

"Okay! Just call from wherever, and I'll come sift you to my house!" Helena screamed.

He wanted to see Matty, but right now, he needed to fix a terrible wrong. He never should've let Sadie go, and if he got her, he didn't intend to let her up for air for at least a few weeks.

Charlotte stood outside of the hotel, panting and trying her best not to pass out. The crazy people— *Oh, God! They think they're vampires!*—hadn't followed her, but they were still inside. *A whole*

room of them! Like some creepy Goth mixer, only they weren't dressed like vampire wannabes. They wore a variety of costumes and everyone she'd met had on bright blue contacts.

Freaky cult people!

But why had she come? She'd known something was weird about that redheaded woman who'd said she was a friend of Sadie's and that she'd put them in touch. "Sadie's in L.A.? My cousin Sadie?" she'd asked. It was only a short drive from Palm Springs, where she lived. Then the woman had placed her hand on her shoulder and stared deeply into her eyes, sending a cold shiver through her body. "The man from your dreams will be at the party," the redhead had said. "He is the one." How the crazy woman knew about her dreams, she didn't know, but this odd tingling in her stomach had told her to take a leap of faith and come to the party. Huge mistake.

Doesn't matter. You're getting out of L.A. and never coming back.

Just then, a man with stylish, short dark hair and deep olive skin pulled up in a very expensive-looking sports car. He got out, and she immediately noticed his tall, lean, muscular frame and expensive suit.

He tossed his keys to the valet and winked his hypnotic aquamarine eyes at her as he passed. He smelled amazing.

She shook her head from side to side, as if

shaking off a dream. *That was weird.* Another valet pulled up behind the man's car with her red Jeep.

"Hi," said a deep male voice from behind her.

She glanced over her shoulder. It was the man.

"My name is Tommaso. Do I know you?" he asked.

That's when she noticed his eyes again. Stunning turquoise-blue eyes. *Oh no! He looks like one of them!*

"Stay away from me!" Charlotte held out her shaking hands.

The man's smile flattened out. "What did I do?"

"You're one of those crazy people! Stay away." She ran to her car, got inside, and screeched out of the parking lot. "Thank God." She couldn't wait to put some serious distance between herself and those people.

She glanced in her rearview mirror. "Oh no."

That Tommaso guy is following me.

Driving as fast as he could and taking only backstreets, Andrus tried calling Sadie several times while on the way to the safe house, but she didn't answer. He honestly couldn't blame her for not taking his call. He wouldn't want to talk to him either.

Please no traffic. Please, gods, let there be no traffic. His heart felt like it might explode from nerves and joy and hope and everything whirling around inside his head. Never in a million years had anyone ever simply walked away from their mate like that, but he had done it without so much as one second of regret. The Universe could not control what was in his heart. It wanted the woman who'd chosen him freely.

Andrus's phone rang, and he hit the speaker. "Yes?"

"Andrus, this is Brutus."

Thank gods. "Brutus, where's Sadie? I need to speak with her."

"She left while I was out walking the dog."

"What do you mean, she left?" Andrus growled.

"Gone."

"Do you know where she went?"

"No."

Fuck. "Okay. Maybe she just went out for an audition. You stay at the house in case she returns."

He ended the call and had an idea. Andrus made a U-turn in the middle of the street.

Less than a half hour later, Andrus pulled up to Sadie's apartment complex. He shut off the engine and ran for the second floor, hopping over the man who still slept in the stairwell.

This place is so charming.

When he got to Sadie's door, he found it cracked open, the sound of muted whimpers and grunts pouring outside. *Fuck. That thing must have her.* The air was permeated with its smell.

He quietly slid his sword from behind his back and then pushed open the door. A man lay on the bed, his arms flailing and scratching at Sadie, who leaned over him.

What the fuck?

"Sadie!" He rushed over and grabbed her shoulders, pulling her off the man.

Sadie looked up at him, her eyes glowing orange like an animal from the fiery pits of hell. *Dear gods!* He released her, and she scrambled back on top of the unconscious man, pushing her mouth over his.

Andrus stood there in shock, unsure of what to do for the first time in his existence. She had been turned into some sort of creature. *Dear fuck, what is she? And how do I stop her?* He couldn't kill her.

He took a deep breath, grabbed his sword with two hands, and smacked her on the back of the head with the hilt. With a loud grunt, she fell to the side, completely out.

Good gods, Sadie. What was done to you? he thought, brushing her brown hair back from her forehead as she lay there next to the man on the bed.

He quickly checked the man, thankful to find a strong pulse. *Your lucky day, buddy.*

He scooped up Sadie in his arms, staring at her beautiful face. *Dear gods, please let there be a way to undo this.*

CHAPTER NINETEEN

Andrus decided that the best bet was to get rid of Brutus and take Sadie back to the safe house, where he'd chain her up in the basement. There, she wouldn't be a danger to anyone while he tried to figure out what to do next. *Was there a cure? What was she? Who had done this?*

He just couldn't believe that this was happening. After everything, this couldn't be her fate. *Some evil, human feeding creature.* He refused to accept that. He refused to believe that fate would be so cruel to him.

Now with Sadie securely chained, he went upstairs and called Cimil. She had to be behind all this or at least know what was going on.

"Andrus, baby! Did you find Sadie?"

"Yes. And I found her feeding on some guy."

"Oh, boy. I guess the cat is out of the bag," Cimil said.

"What cat are you speaking of? And tell me everything—no more lies—or I swear on my life I will hunt you down and ensure you suffer for eternity."

"Whoa, whoa, whoa there, Andy the Awful; I tried to warn you. Sadie is not the woman for you. I wasn't lying."

"Cimil! Tell me what you know! What happened to her!" he yelled.

"She was born, Andrus, that's what happened to her. She's an evil succubus who loves to feed on tasty, innocent mortals."

He felt like the wind had been knocked out of him. "Did you say 'succubus'?"

"Um, yeah. I did. Hello? Does someone need a hearing aid?"

"But the gods sent their kind back to hell and then sealed off their portal." Immortal folklore said that the incubi used their portal to travel home and replace their human shells once they wore out from all that toxic energy they carried around. With no way to do that, any who remained in the human world eventually grew old. Once the physical body died, the incubus became inert, its soul trapped in this world for eternity.

"A few got through our nets," Cimil admitted, "but Sadie's father won't live forever. Neither will she, but they do live a very, very long time."

No, this just couldn't be right. "She...she...they were attacking her."

"Nuh-uh-uh," Cimil sang. "Sadie was feeding off them. Of course, once fed on, the human can't get enough. They just keep on comin' back for more, offering themselves up like a platter of yummy people treats to the evil one. Then they usually go insane and kill themselves after a while if the succubus doesn't kill them first. That Tim guy, for example, made his exit off a bridge."

"She's been lying to me the entire time?" How could he have missed it?

"No, Andy baby. She doesn't remember when she's...you know, not her sucky self. And her incugenes only manifested recently. She has no clue."

No. This can't be. She so nice and wonderful and—"How is this possible, Cimil? How? And why didn't you say anything?"

"Tell *you*? Andrus the Annihilator? You were born to hunt down evil creatures like Sadie. Besides, she's completely harmless when she's in her human state."

"But...but...I love her."

"Sorry. Can't help you there, big guy. I tried to hook you up with the good version, Charlotte, but did you listen to me? Noo...And thanks, by the way, because Zac and I don't get credit for making a match, so he's one step closer to going all mass murderer on us."

He didn't care about Zac; he cared about Sadie. "So both Sadie and Charlotte are succubae?"

"Duh. No. Charlotte's human, but they look alike—their mothers were twins. Sadie's dear old dad is the incubus, which was why Sadie's mom split after she learned the truth. Guess not everyone is cut out for life in the suck-lane. Get it?" She snorted. "Suck. Lane! Dang, I crack myself up."

Dear gods, he was going to kill her. She was completely enjoying this moment of his ultimate suffering. "Why hasn't Sadie's father been executed, Cimil?"

"Hey. He's not a bad guy. He's all settled down, a dentist now. Feeds quietly off his wife and a few preselected nasty people every once in a while. He's mostly harmless. For an incubus. It's a shame about Sadie, though. He'd hoped since she's a hybrid, her naughty side would remain dormant. Now, I don't know what I'm going to tell the poor guy. I'd promised to keep an eye on her while she was out here."

He simply couldn't believe it, yet the signs had been there all along. The strange smell when she transformed, the scratches and bite marks—all defensive wounds from her snacks—and the fact that she'd accepted the immortal news with such ease. It was all because the woman was part demon.

A sexy she-devil. On some level, he'd known all along. *But how is this possible? She's so...so...wonderful.* Not to mention sexy as hell, the kind of sexy that required no effort. She simply oozed it. *Yes, it is in her nature.*

He pressed his palm to his forehead. "You knew all along, didn't you, Cimil? You knew this would happen. I'm going to fucking kill you!"

"No. I didn't know this would happen. You were supposed to fall for Charlotte. Did I not say that ten times? Jeez—hold on. Zac! Get the fire extinguisher! Belch lit the bar on fire again," she screamed. "Hey, Andrus, I gotta go. Some of us have bigger issues to deal with, like ending Zac's sentence before he turns into the biggest mass murderer ever known and the Universe falling off its axis during an immortal mixer that is turning into a giant orgy—Hey! You two. Get a room! And you three, too! For fuck's sake, we can't take you anywhere, K'ak!" she belted out. "Andrus, this shit's getting real. Clothes are coming off—Belch! Get your dick out of that man's cocktail!"

"But I don't know what to do," Andrus said.

"You should've thought of that before you chucked away your chance at happiness for a ruthless predator."

"So why in the world did you put Sadie and I together?" None of this made sense.

"Uhhh...I can't remember. Oh, wait. I know. Because I can't help doing evil things on a subconscious level; meanwhile I'm really trying to do the right thing? Nooo...maybe that's not it. Wait. I've got it! You needed help with Charlotte and my Spidey senses told me Sadie could help you tap into that mushy side women love. I wasn't wrong. But I guess I was." She snorted. "Weird, right?"

"I knew I shouldn't have trusted you," he said.

"Well, next time, you should listen to you. Especially before falling in love with a female who will be hunted down for killing innocent mortals."

His stomach and heart filled with a dread so vile

and heavy, he could barely breathe. "How many has she killed?"

"About twelve—I stopped counting. But she's been snacking on her co-workers for months. Plus a few producers. And her landlord. She's really gettin' around. Which is why if I weren't so evil, I would've turned her in already. But because I'm also good, I am compelled to protect those pesky humans and must take this opportunity to remind you of your oath, dear demigod."

Fuck. No. No. No. This can't be happening. "I won't kill her."

"But you swore an oath to the gods," she argued. "You swore to kill evil creatures who feed on Forbiddens."

Humans who had good souls and auras were called "Forbiddens" because it was forbidden to harm them. They were essentially a protected class. For those who were rotten—violent criminals, rapists, pedophiles, etc.—they were fair prey for human feeders like vampires.

"What if I refuse to kill her?" Andrus asked.

"Then it's only a question of time before someone else catches her. Sucks to be a succubus. Tootles."

The call ended, and he looked down at his feet, panic setting in. *Oh fuck.* They would be coming for her. The Uchben like Brutus or perhaps Votan, the God of Death and War. But they would come for her eventually. She had killed innocent mortals.

And you've sworn an oath to always protect mankind from evil predators like the one in the basement.

What the hell am I going to do?

Sadie awoke in a dark room that smelled of dampness, chained to a bed, the cold steel biting at her wrists and ankles. "What the hell?"

Oh no. The monster finally caught me. Oh, God. Oh, God. Her eyes searched the darkness for any clue as to where she might be or a way out.

How the hell did I even get here?

The last thing she remembered was going through her stuff at her place, before heading off to the airport, when her sleazy landlord showed up demanding payment. Only, he wasn't asking for money, because her bill had been settled by Andrus. Oh no, that jerk off wanted her to jerk him off.

Asshole! But what had happened? She didn't remember a thing. *It's officially freak the hell out time.*

She gave a little tug on her chains. *Shit.* There was only an inch or two of give and not nearly enough to get any sort of leverage. *I'm going to die.*

The lonely dangling light bulb above flickered on, and she held her breath, her body burning with adrenaline. Now, with the lights on, she could see she was in someone's basement—stairs off to the corner, a boiler, and some boxes piled up against the wall.

"Hello?" she said, her voice trembling with fear. "I don't know who you are, but you're making a huge mistake. My friends aren't the sort of people you want to fuck with, and they'll come looking for me."

They probably wouldn't, but what did she have to lose?

Heavy footsteps descended the stairs, and when she spotted those familiar leather pants, she wanted to scream with joy. "Andrus! Ohmygod, you found me!"

He stopped at the foot of the bed, his aquamarine eyes burning with anger and a sword in one hand.

Her moment of joy turned to terror. "Andrus, free me."

"I am sorry, Sadie, but I cannot do that."

"What the fuck, Andrus. Does this have anything to do with *her*? I mean, I know you said your feelings for me would change, but this is a little extreme."

"Charlotte, who is your cousin by the way, has nothing to do with this."

She blinked at him, straining to keep her head elevated. "Charlotte? You mean your Charlotte is my cousin?"

He nodded coldly. "Yes."

"But how?"

"Small world, I suppose."

"Fine. Whatever. But why've you chained me up?" she panted her words.

Andrus propped his sword against the wall and turned to face her, his jaw pumping with tension. Suddenly, he grabbed the hem of his black tee and pulled it over his head, revealing his menacing pecs and biceps and the deep grooves of those rock-hard abs.

"Wha-what are you doing?" she asked.

He kicked off his boots and then began unzipping his pants, a sinister look in his feral eyes. "What does it look like?" he said, in that deep, ominous voice.

"Andrus, I don't know what's going on, but you're scaring me."

He shed his pants, standing completely nude to her side, his long thick cock harder than hell.

"Andrus. No. I mean it."

He ignored her completely and then reached for her jeans, quickly peeling them down and exposing her lower torso. "No, no, no. You don't want to do this," she begged.

"Let's just see about that."

Everything went black.

When Sadie came to again, Andrus lay on his back on the cement floor, naked, bleeding from deep scratches all over his torso, face, and rib cage. And...

A huge fucking smile plastered on his face?

She still had the cuffs on her wrists and ankles, but the chains that had held her to the bed were broken.

She looked down at her shredded pile of clothes on the floor. She, too, was completely nude.

Oh fuck. Oh fuck. What's going on? She grabbed Andrus's tee from the floor and slipped it over her head. On her, it was like a minidress.

She turned to sprint for the stairs when she heard his voice. "Wait! Don't go."

She glanced over her shoulder.

"Watch the video," he grumbled, pointing to a camera in the corner.

"You filmed us? You raped me and filmed us?" She ran for his sword and pushed the point against his heart.

Andrus held up his hands. "What? Rape? Gods no, woman. The chains were to protect me."

"From what?"

"From you, but it didn't work. Watch the video." He slowly staggered to his feet and slid on his leather pants, wincing with every movement.

"What are you talking about?"

He looked at her with a hard expression. "All those times you woke up with scratches and bites, those were defensive wounds from your supper."

"I don't understand."

"No one has been hunting you, Sadie. You're the predator. A succubus—a half-breed, anyway."

"You drag me down here to your basement, chain me, I wake up naked, and you expect me to listen to your crazy lies."

"I would never, ever hurt you. And I think in your heart you know it. Watch the video." He gestured toward the camera on the tripod.

She slowly walked over to the camera, still pointing the sword at him. It was still rolling, so she hit the stop and rewind button.

She hit play and the scene unfolded in a blur of unbelievable images: She screamed for her life as Andrus peeled down her jeans. Then he stepped away from her as her eyes glowed bright orange, and she snapped her chains like ropes made of licorice. She pounced and took him down like a cheetah snagging a baby deer.

She covered her mouth. "Oh shit." She watched in horror as this thing that looked like her straddled Andrus and had her way with him, clawing at his chest and riding his cock. Then the two of them began rolling around on the cold floor, fucking like savage animals.

Sadie's eyes darted over to Andrus and then back at the camera. "That's—that's us?"

He nodded with a cocky triumphant smile. "Oh yeah. And it was so fucking hot. You have no idea."

"But I don't understand."

He approached her slowly, as if she were a

hungry lion he didn't want to provoke. "I caught you sucking the life from a man in your apartment, and I had to knock you over the head to keep you from killing him."

She gasped. "I almost killed Mr. Blakely, my landlord?"

He nodded.

"Please don't tell me I had sex with him, too?"

"From what I could see, you were merely draining his life force."

She walked over to the bed and plopped down. "I don't understand."

Andrus sat next to her. "Cimil says your father is an incubus."

Her head whipped up. "My dad?"

"He likely would've kept it hidden from you for your own safety. Your kind are not welcome in the human world. You're very dangerous."

"But I've never seen him do anything strange." Except that her mother had left them all so suddenly and never came back. Perhaps she found out the truth and was afraid of them.

"You can ask him when you're ready," Andrus said. "But you just saw the proof on that tape, which is why I made it; so you could see for yourself. That, and I needed to see it with my own eyes, too."

Oh God. "I think I'm going to be sick. I'm a monster."

"When I learned the truth, I thought so, too. But

then I realized what a strange thing fate is."

She looked up into his loving eyes. How could he stand the sight of her?

"My first mate truly was a monster. Her hate of life and humanity ran soul deep. But being with her, as strange and horrific as it was, taught me the difference between true evil and those who are simply struggling to be good despite their genetics."

"You can't possibly be saying I'm good."

He made a little grumble and ran his hands through his messy fuck-styled hair. "This is the problem. You are good when you're in this form, but when you turn, you're not. And apparently you've killed quite a few people."

She cupped her hands over her mouth in horror. "I have?"

He nodded. "So I am told."

Her heart sank. This couldn't be happening. She was like Dr. Jekyll and Mr. Hyde. "What am I going to do? I don't want to kill people."

"Nor do the gods wish this, which is why they will send someone to kill you."

"What? I'm going to die?" On the other hand, maybe it was for the best. She was a killer.

He cupped her cheek and gazed lovingly into her eyes. "I will never let anyone harm you as long as I exist."

"I'm evil, Andrus. Evil and dangerous."

He slowly reached for her cheek and brushed his

thumb over her bottom lip. "Which is why fate could not have chosen better. I am fairly skilled at handling evil, dangerous creatures, so I will find a way to help you control your urges." He grinned. "I love you, Sadie."

"You do?"

"What about Charlotte?" she asked.

He shrugged. "She looks just like you, but she's nothing like you."

"What about Matty?"

"I'll simply have to trust that the Universe will find a way to make things right. But I can't deny my heart. Not anymore. Not when there's you."

Tears filled her eyes. She didn't know what to say or make of this or how to possibly understand what she'd just learned, but Andrus was the only thing she could see clearly in the surrounding storm.

"I love you, too, Andrus." She leaned in and planted a big kiss on his bad-boy pouty lips.

He pulled away. "I'm glad. Because you and I are going to have to put up a fight to make our destiny."

CHAPTER TWENTY

Andrus had a plan. A very bad plan, but it was the only one he could come up with. And with the looming threat of the immortal community finding out about Sadie—a banned species—he had to attack the problem head-on and hope for the best. Because plan B, living on the run, wasn't a long-term solution. The gods could easily find them.

Early in the morning, he walked through the lobby toward the ballroom at the Beverly Hills Hotel with Sadie, gripping her hand firmly in his. He'd stayed up all night making arrangements and calling every ex-Demilord (now all demigods like himself) he could get his hands on. They were no longer under his command, as they'd all been freed, but they still remained loyal to him.

This is either going to go really well, or really bad.

He glanced down at Sadie in her little pink summer dress and gave her a comforting smile. "Do you trust me?"

She nodded. "Of course. But why won't you tell me your plan?"

Because I don't know if you'll agree.

"All you need to know is that I love you. And there's nothing I wouldn't do for you."

She let out a breath. "Okay. Let's do this, then."

They opened the doors to the ballroom and entered with a gasp.

"Dear gods," he whispered. "I will need to have my brain washed."

Nude, sleeping people lie everywhere—over the tables, on top of the bar, on the floor—in various states of postcoital dress. Empty bottles, confetti, clothes, condoms, and food littered every corner.

"This must've been one wild party," Sadie said.

"It's about to get wilder," he said.

᠊ᡦᠥᠥᡦ᠊

What is he up to? Sadie thought as Andrus began clapping his hands and screaming at the room full of hungover partygoers. "Everybody wake up!"

The doors flung open behind them and in walked ten huge, menacing-looking men in black leather pants, black T-shirts, and leather dusters. They all wore dark sunglasses, but if she had to guess, she'd bet they had turquoise eyes.

"Friends of yours?" she asked Andrus.

"They are my brothers," he replied and dipped his head at the gang of biker-looking dudes. "Thanks for coming."

One of the men, a taller guy with longer dark hair, dipped his head. "Anything for you, sir. Where would you like us to start?"

"I want you to guard this succubus," Andrus

replied. "Don't let anyone lay a finger on her."

The man looked past Sadie. "What succubus? And why would we guard one versus killing her?"

Andrus pointed right at her. "Gentlemen, may I introduce Sadie. The woman I have chosen to be mine."

They blinked and rumbled a few words between them.

"Are you sure about this, sir?" the taller guy said.

"Yes, and I am taking full responsibility for her actions."

"Andrus, you know there is nothing we wouldn't do for you, but—"

"I freed you all," Andrus interjected. "And you all swore fealty to me. So under the laws of the immortals, your fealty must also extend to my wife."

Wife?

"Andrus?" Sadie said. "What are you doing?"

He turned toward her and smiled reassuringly. "Sadie, I've only known you for all of eight days, but there is no doubt in my heart that you are the one. You've made me angry, you've mesmerized me with your beauty, you've helped me remember who I once was and brought my heart back to life. If that's not enough, there's the fact that I rejected my mate for you, which is unheard of in our world. I love you, with my free heart, and I want you to be my wife."

A tall, statuesque woman with an enormous beehive on her head stepped toward them from the awakening crowd. *Holy shit.* There were real bees swarming around her head and crawling on her body.

"What is the meaning of thisss, Andruzzz?" she said with a buzzy lisp.

"Colel." Andrus dipped his head. "Lovely to see you again, Mistress of Bees. I am interrupting your very horrible hangover to marry this succubus."

A naked man with ankle-length silver and black hair, who wore an enormous silver headdress with intertwining serpents, stepped from the crowd. "The gods have declared any of her kind to be executed on the spot."

Andrus held up his hand. "K'ak, also a pleasure to see you again."

Did he just call that guy "cock"?

Andrus continued, "I am going to marry this woman who, as everyone can clearly see for themselves, has a good aura. She is a Forbidden."

"She is a demon who feeds off of Forbiddens," argued the headdress-cock-guy.

"She is half human and that half is good. Just look at her," Andrus insisted.

The crowd of about one hundred people grumbled in agreement.

Could everyone in the room really see her aura?

"And when she shifts into her other form, which is not so good, what then, Demilord?" Brutus stepped from the crowd, holding a long gleaming sword in one hand and the elderly cocker spaniel in the other.

Wow. Brutus speaks? And he looked like he wanted to kill her.

"She will learn to control herself with the right help," said a deep familiar voice.

Sadie turned her head and spotted a familiar-looking face. "Daddy? What are you doing here?" He wore a dark gray suit that matched both his hair and the very pissed-off look on his face.

"Do you think I would let my little girl be hunted like some animal?" her father said.

"Move!" Cimil barked from behind him, pushing an extra-extra-long stroller. "Make way for the evil seeds." *What the hell is that woman wearing?* It was a giant blue teddy bear costume.

"Cimil?" Andrus said, sounding unsure if he was happy to see her or scared as hell.

"Okay, everyone," Cimil said. "I'm gonna just lay it all out on the table. I fucked this one up. Majorly. Andrus is not supposed to be with that sucky succubus."

"Cimil!" Andrus looked like he was about to lunge for her when she threw out her hands.

"Hold your balls, Andrus. I'm not finished yet." He stared at her and she stared back. "No. I really mean it. I'd love to see you hold them."

Andrus's expression was somewhere between confused and livid.

"No?" Cimil said. "Not gonna drop leather trow for me?" She shrugged. "Okay, fine. Anyway, where was I? Oh yeah. I was about to tell everyone that I've recently learned that the last apocalypse sorta changed all the rules."

"What do you mean, Ziiimil?" buzzed the beehive lady.

"I have absolutely no clue," replied Cimil. "All I know is that since our very close call, everything has felt off, chaotic, like the lines of good and bad and right and wrong are all jumbled up."

"This is no reason to allow an incubus and a succubus to walk the earth, tormenting Forbiddens. They are evil," argued the cock-guy.

"That's the point," Cimil interjected. "It's the piece I couldn't figure out. This guy," she pointed to Sadie's father, "is supposed to be evil, and he once was. But now he does root canals and is in a loving committed relationship. And these little guys," she started blowing kisses to the four tiny carriages in front of her, "were supposed to be born good, but are obviously tiny demons who will likely cause mass destruction once they're old enough to drive."

"They're your children; I do not think it's a surprise to anyone that they are evil," interjected another familiar male face in the crowd. Sadie recognized him from Cimil's office—depressing black hair and beautiful turquoise eyes.

"I'm telling you, something is happening," Cimil

said. "And if you don't want to believe me, talk to my Maaskab babysitter. He'll tell you he can't stop thinking about doing nice things. It's driving him crazy."

"You have a Maaskab coming to your home?" Brutus growled.

"Sorry, everyone. You can either fight it or accept it. But it's a new world order. And evil is the new good."

The room rumbled with skepticism. As for herself, she had no clue what any of this really meant—heck, she was still reeling from the fact that her father had come all the way to L.A. and put himself at risk. And that he was an incubus. And that she was half-succubus. *Jesus, my life is a mess.* But at least she had Andrus.

"Cimil," Andrus said, "I have to ask, then, what does that mean? What will happen to those of us who are good?"

"My dead-peeps are telling me that anyone who doesn't have a special someone to ground them is gonna flip out or go to the...dark side," she said in a Darth Vader voice. "Which now explains why I had a vision of Zac going on a slaughter spree. He will be one of many to change." She sighed. "Ah, the Universe and her sense of humor. You gotta, gotta love it."

"No, I don't," Andrus replied, "but I do love Sadie, and from the sound of it, the sooner we marry, the better." He turned to Sadie. "If you'll have me?"

She gazed up into his loving turquoise eyes. She felt like her entire world had flipped upside down, but she knew this was the man she was meant to be with. "Can we live in L.A. so I can still be an actress?"

He cupped her face. "Anything for you, Sadie. You just cannot suck the life force from any more producers or co-workers, or anyone else, for that matter. Just me. And me only."

That sounded kind of nice. Especially if she got to use that big straw of his when she did the sucking. *Oh, God. Did I just think that?*

"Thank you, Andrus. I would've said yes anyway, but it's good to know that I don't have to give up my dreams just because I'm half evil."

Andrus leaned down and kissed her lips softly. "You saw that tape. You're more than just a little evil, and I wouldn't have it any other way."

"All right, kids." Cimil clapped her hands. "Who wants to play minister?"

A man in a pair of white underwear, with long hair and a beer belly, stumbled forward. "I wanna marry them," he slurred.

"Who's that?" Sadie whispered to Andrus.

"The God of Wine and Intoxication, and considering the other options in the room, I think we should accept his offer."

Sadie looked at the people, who were mostly

naked, standing around chatting and drinking without a care in the world.

"Okay. He's got underwear on. I'll take him."

CHAPTER TWENTY-ONE

Chained to the bed with deity-reinforced steel chains—a wedding gift from the gods—Sadie lay nervously waiting for Andrus in his safe house bedroom.

"But what if I break them again?" she called out.

Andrus entered the room, shirtless and carrying two glasses of champagne. He looked so damned sexy with his light olive skin, hard chiseled pecs, and ripped abs. She couldn't believe this sexy huge man was now her husband. And holy cow. He'd picked out one heck of a diamond ring for her. The wedding bands, however, would have to wait. He said he wanted to have them made in Russia when they went to visit his castle after their honeymoon, which, by the way, would be on some private island near Greece that belonged to one of the gods. They'd leave tomorrow morning. Anyway, yes, Andrus had a castle. That was pretty cool, though she couldn't wait to see the merry-go-round he kept in the basement. Andrus told her he'd purchased it from an old Russian circus, hoping his children would enjoy it someday. That man was a closet romantic if she ever met one. Who would've guessed it?

"You might break free," he replied, giving her chains one more test tug, "but we've already proven I can handle your more kinky side."

"So why do I turn in the first place?" she asked.

"My best guess? You just get hungry. So I plan to keep you well fed. It's the same technique vampires use to stay out of trouble."

"You're also immortal," she said, "which means I have an endless food supply." They really were perfect for each other. In fact, during the ceremony, she began to get this strange feeling in the pit of her stomach, and it wasn't the fact that a huge drunk guy in white underwear—who was actually quite attractive despite the slurring and beer belly—was marrying them. It all felt a little too perfect, like it was meant to be. And when she looked over at Cimil, the goddess gave her a wicked little wink. Was it possible that she'd planned this entire thing?

After the ceremony, while Andrus was busy being congratulated by his friends, she cornered Cimil. There was one loose thread she couldn't let go of: this other man. Cimil had said that Sadie was meant to fall in love with someone else.

"Who is he, Cimil?" Sadie had asked.

Cimil gave her a look. "Oh, Sippy. You've been married for two minutes, and you're already on the hunt? Wow. You succubae really are little sluts."

Sippy. She finally got the joke, but... "No. What is the matter with you? I just want to be sure I stay clear of him. I don't want anything getting between me and Andrus."

Cimil grinned. "He's actually here in this room right now, staring at you and wondering why all of the good ones are taken."

"He is?" Sadie's eyes had swept the crowd—yes, still mostly naked. Immortals were so weird—seeing if anyone gave off a vibe.

"Yes," Cimil had replied. "And if you don't feel him in your heart, it's because your heart is spoken for. The Universe has her way. She's a smart one." Cimil poked her temple. "Just like you were smart enough to only gobble on evil people."

"Really? But I thought you said I'd killed a bunch of Forbiddens?"

Cimil had laughed wickedly, shrugged, and walked away.

Sadie knew she'd never feel good about killing anyone, but it was better knowing that her actions while in her altered state might not have been as horrific as she'd thought.

So now, she was happier than hell. And with Andrus's and her father's help, she'd learn how to control herself. Lessons would begin after their trip to Russia and honeymoon.

In the meantime, she and Andrus had a little matter that needed attention.

"But I want to remember," she said, feeling like this was her first time having sex, her stomach all flutters and knots.

"We shall take it slow. I promise." He unbuttoned his pants and slid them down, freeing his hard, thick and very ready shaft.

Dear gods, he looks so good. She just wanted to eat him up and not just in a succubus kind of way. "Wait. Please tell me you brought condoms."

Andrus held out his hand and a roll of XXL gold-wrapped squares dropped down, dangling all the way to the floor. "I will manage my plow until you find a more effective way to protect your field."

My hero. "Or until we're ready to share our life with little demons of our own." For the time being, though, she wanted to focus on Andrus and only Andrus. The guy really, really deserved some dedicated attention. She'd gotten to meet the infamous Helena, Niccolo, and Matty at the wedding—they'd sifted in right in the middle. But she could see how much they loved each other and why Andrus might want that for himself. Well, she was going to give him a whole lotta love.

He rolled on a condom and then went straight for her little dress, making a deep, throaty groan as he lifted the hem and tore away her panties. "Mmmm…" he said, brushing his hand between her legs with a few teasing strokes. "Maybe we can do slow later."

She nodded her head, already panting with arousal. "Good idea. Just be sure to stop if I start to turn."

"Oh no. There will be no stopping once we start,

so you'll just have to control yourself." He nestled himself between her thighs, spreading her legs as wide as they could go. "Are you ready?"

Feeling her core throbbing and aching with need, she panted out a yes.

Staring into her eyes, gripping his shaft, he thrust himself into her. She gasped and threw back her head, relishing the sensation of his cock pushing forward. She gripped the chains around her wrists, biting back a deep groan and any thoughts of orgasming. She didn't want it to end quickly, but he felt so good inside her—hot, velvety, and large.

He bent his head away from her lips and kissed his way down her neck and collarbone. He then tore away the front of her dress, exposing her breasts. When his mouth began sucking her nipple, she bowed her back, offering as much as she could to him. Meanwhile, his hips, those delicious male hips pumped and ground, pumped and ground, hitting her c-spot over and over again.

She rocked her hips to increase the sensual pleasure, but the better it felt, the hotter she grew. "No. I'm leaving you, Andrus. I don't want to."

Pillaring one arm to the side of her head, his other hand cupped her cheek as he stared deeply into her eyes. "Then don't go. Stay here with me."

With their eyes locked together, she felt every inch of Andrus moving in and out of her body.

"That's right," he said in a deep gruff voice filled

with sinful sex. "Stay here. Just me and you." He kissed her hard for several long minutes and then returned to her eyes; meanwhile his hips thrust, slamming his balls against the base of her entrance.

The sensation of him sliding his hot hard flesh into her, his body pushing all the right buttons was too much. She couldn't hold back any longer.

She let go and screamed his name, meeting every push of his hips with hard movements of her own. The orgasm slammed into her, igniting her body like a fuse that started from the inside out.

"Oh, gods. Fuck me. Harder, harder, Andrus," she urged him on as her release washed over her in an unrelenting wave of delicious jabs and tingles and contractions. Meanwhile, he rode her hard, fucking her like a beast chasing a state of utter euphoria.

Andrus threw back his head and groaned loudly toward the sky, spilling his cum.

With one final thrust of his hips, Andrus let out a forced breath and then dropped his head to her collarbone, panting like he'd just run a marathon. "Fuck. Me."

"I think I just did," she said, barely able to catch her breath or think straight. She was just so glad he could go all night, because she'd be ready for another round in about two minutes. It was just that toe-curling good.

"Did you really walk away from your mate for me?" She couldn't believe how lucky she was.

Still inside her, he lifted his eyes to meet hers. "My heart was already spoken for."

"I love you," she said.

He kissed her softly and withdrew. "I think it's time for that body licking I promised."

"Oh yes. I'd like that very much, but I'm also feeling kind of hungry." She grinned, remembering how much he'd enjoyed her wild side on that video.

He smiled with his sexy swollen lips. "Dinner is served."

"And you look delicious."

CHAPTER TWENTY-TWO

"Dammit, Tula, overalls and turtleneck? Must you torment me so, woman?" Zac growled from behind his desk, trying to sort through the surveys taken after the mixer. It seemed they had only managed to produce eight official mated couples that night, which was completely ridiculous when not one person went home without getting lucky. Even Cimil's unicorn had a little fun with one of the uninvited sex faeries who'd showed up.

"Mr. Zac," Tula said, parking her hand on her hip, carrying a bunch of files in the other, "it's casual Friday."

"Yes, I am aware." It was the reason he'd not bothered wearing a shirt to work.

You're so full of shit. You just wanted an excuse to show Tula your badass immortal pecs and abs.

He went on, "However, I've told you before: you cannot wear such clothing around me. Now either you'll need to come to work dressed in the appropriately slutty attire, or I will have to dismiss you. Are we clear?"

She sighed and shook her head. "Mr. Zac, I swear you gods have a few marbles loose, but if it will make you happy and help you concentrate..." She set down her files on her desk just a few feet from his and unhooked the straps of her overalls. They slid down her body and pooled on the floor. "There. Is that better?"

Holy saints of sexiness! His cock sprang up like a Jack in the box, producing a very painful erection against his leather pants. "You're—you're," he swallowed, "wearing granny panties. Dear gods, woman, what are you trying to do to me?"

She rolled her eyes. "You're hopeless, Mr. Zac."

"You must remove them immediately, or I fear I won't ever be able to stand again."

She shook her head. "Aren't you the funny one." She walked away toward the breakroom area, strutting her sweet little ass and those huge, huge flowered panties.

No, I'm serious. Gah, my cock.

His cell phone rang on his desk, and he picked it up, welcoming the distraction. "Zac here," he groaned.

"Zac, it's Tommaso." The man sounded distressed.

"Tommaso? What is the matter?"

"Is it true about what Cimil said at the party?"

"Which thing? I try to forget anything my sister says," Zac replied.

"She said that we would start turning evil unless we get mated."

Ah yes. That. He definitely didn't want to think about turning into a murderer unless, like everyone else who was single, he found his mate. Either way, it would suck for him. He loved being single. *I wish Cimil had been right the first time when she thought I was going to go nuts from being banished too long.* At least then, he'd had a chance at real freedom by merely serving his sentence.

"Yes," Zac replied, "it is true—she said that. Why?"

"I think it's happening already. My eyes have changed to black. They're not blue anymore."

What the fuck? "Are you certain you haven't been eating some of K'ak's magic brownies?" K'ak, one of the other gods, thought it would be funny to bring some to the party. Of course, that was over a week ago, so it would be strange for the effects to kick in so soon. The brownies usually took effect at the most inopportune moments about a month or so after consumption. Not funny at all.

"No." Tommaso panted. "I did not eat any fucking brownies."

"This is not good at all." If Tommaso was right, the change could be happening to others already, too. "The problem is I think I found my mate," Tommaso added.

"Oh. Well, you see, there's some good news," Zac said. "Now you simply need her to accept you."

"That's the issue. I found her tied up in my closet. I apparently kidnapped her."

"You are correct; that does not sound like a positive thing. Why would you do that, Tommaso?"

"I don't know. But I untied her and she ran. The

last thing I remember, I was chasing her and then I found myself sitting in a 7-Eleven parking lot, covered in blood and black stuff. It's even in my fucking hair."

Zac swallowed. *Holy saints, is Tommaso turning into a Maaskab?* It sure the hell sounded like it. *Dear gods, this is not good.* "Text me the address, we're coming to get you."

"Please hurry." Tommaso ended the call.

"Tula!" Zac called, and she came scurrying from the break room in her giant underwear, which he tried desperately to ignore.

"Yes? What's the matter?" she asked.

"Get your clothes back on. It's time for you to get your hands dirty."

"What do you mean?" she asked.

"I may need you to help me capture a Maaskab."

TO BE CONTINUED...

AUTHOR'S NOTE

Hi All!

I hope you enjoyed book #1 of the new series. Each story will be about a new couple, with a teaser for the next story at the end—so not exactly a dreaded cliffhanger and easy to read as standalones. Obviously, the next victim will be Tommaso (May 2016)! More info, including preorder links, can be found here:

www.mimijean.net/immortal_matchmakers.html

After that, I have the following stories planned:

— BRUTUS
— COLEL, the Mistress of Bees
— THE GOD OF WINE
— THE GODDESS OF FORGETFULNESS

Don't forget, if you want a signed Immortal Matchmakers bookmark, shoot your mailing address to: mimi@mimijean.net. (I still personally answer all of my emails.) Be SURE to mention if you POST A REVIEW because I'll include some surprise "thank you" swag, too. (It's on a first come basis, but I usually have some sort of goodies on hand!)

As always, I want to thank you for reading my books! I'm constantly blown away by everyone's supportiveness and willingness to take these crazy journeys with me. It seriously makes being a writer so, so fun because I get to go where my heart takes me. (Who's up for my next story FUGLY, coming in late Sept! See blurb here in the back.)

Thank you again, from the bottom of my heart!

Happy Reading,

Mimi

P.S. If you're looking for more fun with the gods, read the series that started it all: ACCIDENTALLY YOURS!

Accidentally in Love with...a God? (Book #1 – the story of Votan, God of Death and War)

Accidentally Married to...a Vampire? (Book #2 – the story of Niccolo, Helena, and Andrus)

Sun God Seeks...Surrogate? (Book #3 – the story of Kinich, the Sun God)

Accidentally...Evil? (a Novella, Book 3.5 – the story of Chaam, the God of Male Virility)

Vampires Need Not...Apply? (Book 4 – the Story of the Goddess of Suicide)

Accidentally...Cimil? (a Novella, Book 4.5 – the story of guess who)

Accidentally...Over? (Series Finale, Book 5 – the story of Máax, the God of Time Travel)

ACKNOWLEDGEMENTS

Thank you to Team Minky, my street team, who is always there to cheer me on with every book release and for all the fun in between. You ladies are incredible!

A HUUUGE thank you to my gods and goddesses who suck it up and read a book that is less than perfect so I can deliver a more awesome story to my readers: Kylie, Dalitza, Bridget, and Ally. And as always, thank you to TEAM MIMI for your professional support in making my books sparkle and shine: Latoya, Pauline, Su, Jan, and Stef!

FUGLY - COMING SOON!

Coming September 28th, 2015

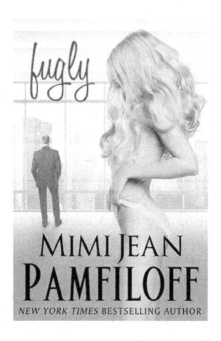

My name is Lily Snow. I am twenty-five years old, and despite being born with an extremely unattractive face, I have never doubted who I am: smart, driven, and beautiful on the inside.

Until I met Maxwell Cole.

He's handsome, excessively wealthy, and the owner of Cole Cosmetics. It's been my dream to work for this man for as long as I can remember.

The good news is he wants to hire me. The bad news is he wants me for all the wrong reasons. Ugly reasons.

In exchange, he's offered me my dreams on a silver platter. The job. The title. A beautiful future. But this man is as messed up and ugly as they come on the inside. I'm not sure anyone can help him, and he just might take my heart down with him.

(STAND ALONE NOVEL)

BUY NOW: www.mimijean.net/fugly.html

MerCiless

Coming November 30th, 2015!
Book #3, The Mermen Trilogy

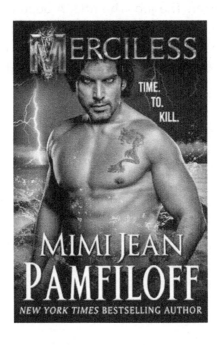

This Guy Messed with the Wrong Woman...

There's a funny thing about luck. One day it runs
out. And when it does you'd better be ready to
answer for your sins. Especially if you are a
merman.

BUY LINKS:
www.mimijean.net/merciless-book-3.html

MACK (from the King Trilogy)

Coming February, 2016

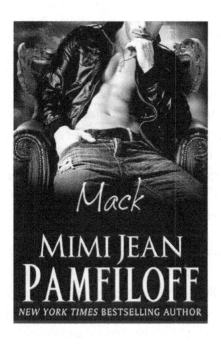

He won't break you. But his story will tear your heart to pieces...

BUY LINKS:
www.mimijean.net/mack.html

Glossary

Black Jade: Found only in a particular mine located in southern Mexico, this jade has very special supernatural properties, including the ability to absorb supernatural energy—in particular, god energy. When worn by humans, it is possible for them to have physical contact with a god. If injected, it can make a person addicted to doing bad things. If the jade is fueled with dark energy and then released, it can be used as a weapon. Chaam personally likes using it to polish his teeth.

Demilords: Once upon a time, they were a group of immortal badass vampires who'd been infused with the light of the gods. Now free from their jobs (killing Obscuros), and their vampire bloodline dead, they have all turned into plain old demigods, but are still just as deadly and lethal as ever.

Maaskab: Originally a cult of bloodthirsty Mayan priests who believed in the dark arts. It is rumored they are responsible for bringing down their entire civilization with their obsession for human sacrifices (mainly young female virgins). Once Chaam started making half-human children, he decided all firstborn males would make excellent

Maaskab due to their proclivity for evil.

Obscuros: Evil vampires who do not live by the Pact and who like to dine on innocent humans since they really do taste the best.

The Pact: An agreement between the gods and good vampires that dictates the dos and don'ts. There are many parts to it, but the most important rules are vampires are not allowed to snack on good people (called Forbiddens), they must keep their existence a secret, and they are responsible for keeping any rogue vampires in check.

Payal: Although the gods can take humans to their realm and make them immortal, Payals are the true genetic offspring of the gods but are born mortal, just like humans. Most do not have any powers.

Uchben: An ancient society of scholars and warriors who serve as the gods' eyes and ears in the human world. They also do the books and manage the gods' earthly assets.

Character Definitions
The Gods

Although every culture around the world has their own names and beliefs related to beings of worship, there are actually only fourteen gods. And since the gods are able to access the human world only through the portals called cenotes, located in the Yucatán, the Mayans were big fans.

Another fun fact: The gods often refer to each other as brother and sister, but the truth is they are just another species of the Creator and completely unrelated.

Acan—God of Wine and Intoxication: Also known as Belch, Acan has been drunk for a few thousand years. He generally wears only tightie whities, but since he's the life of the party, he's been known to mix it up and go naked, too. Whatever works.

Ah-Ciliz—God of Solar Eclipses: Called A.C. by his brethren, Ah-Ciliz is generally thought of as a giant buzz kill because of his dark attitude.

Akna—Goddess of Fertility: She is so powerful, it is

said she can make inanimate objects fornicate and that anyone who gets in the same room as her ends up pregnant. She is often seen hanging out with her brother Acan at parties.

Backlum Chaam—God of Male Virility: He's responsible for discovering black jade and figuring out how to procreate with humans.

Camaxtli—Goddess of the Hunt: Also once known as Fate until she was discovered to be a fake and had her powers stripped away by the Universe. She's now referred to as "Fake."

Colel Cab—Mistress of Bees: Though she has many, many powers, "Bees" is most known for the live beehive hat on her head. She has never had a boyfriend or lover because her bees get too jealous.

Goddess of Forgetfulness: She has no official name that is known of and has the power to make anyone forget anything. She spends her evenings DJing because she finds the anonymity of dance clubs to be comforting.

Ixtab—Goddess of Happiness (ex-Goddess of Suicide): Ixtab's once morbid frock used to make children scream. But since finding her soul mate, she's now the epitome of all things happy.

K'ak (Pronounced "cock"): The history books remember him as K'ak Tiliw Chan Yopaat, ruler of Copán in the 700s AD. King K'ak is one of Cimil's favorite brothers. We're not really sure what he does, but he can throw bolts of lightning, wears a giant silver and jade headdress with intertwining serpents, and has long black and silver hair.

Kinich Ahau—ex-God of the Sun: Known by many other names, depending on the culture, Kinich likes to go by Nick these days. He's also now a vampire—something he's actually not so bummed about. He is mated to the love of his life, Penelope, the Ruler of the House of Gods.

Máax—Once known as the God of Truth, Máax was banished for repeatedly violating the ban on time travel. However, since helping to save the world from the big "over," he is now known as the God of Time Travel. Also turns out he was the God of Love, but no one figured that out until his mate, Ashli, inherited his power. Ashli is now the fourteenth deity, taking the place of Camaxtli, the Fake.

Votan—God of Death and War: Also known as Odin, Wotan, Wodan, God of Drums (he has no idea how the hell he got that title; he hates drums), and Lord of Multiplication (okay, he is pretty darn good at math so that one makes sense). These days, Votan goes by Guy Santiago (it's a long story—read ACCIDENTALLY IN LOVE WITH...A

GOD?), but despite his deadly tendencies, he's all heart.

Yum Cimil—Goddess of the Underworld: Also known as Ah-Puch by the Mayans, Mictlantecuhtli (try saying that one ten times) by the Aztec, Grim Reaper by the Europeans, Hades by the Greeks...you get the picture! Despite what people say, Cimil is actually a female, adores a good bargain (especially garage sales) and the color pink, and she hates clowns. She's also bat-shit crazy, has an invisible pet unicorn named Minky, and is married to Roberto, the king of all vampires.

Zac Cimi—Bacab of the North: What the heck is a Bacab? According to the gods' folklore, the Bacabs are the four eldest and most powerful of the gods. Once thought to be the God of Love, we now know differently. Zac is the God of Temptation, and his tempting ways have landed him in very hot water. Because no matter how tempting your brother's mate might be, trying to steal her is wrong. He is currently serving time in Los Angeles with Cimil, running the Immortal Matchmakers agency.

Not the Gods

Andrus: Ex-Demilord (vampire who's been given the gods' light), now just a demigod after his maker, the vampire queen, died. According to Cimil, his son (who hasn't been born yet) is destined to marry Helena and Niccolo's daughter, Matty.

Brutus: One of the gods' elite Uchben warriors. He doesn't speak much, but that's because he and his team are telepathic. They are also immortal (a gift from the gods) and next in line to be Uchben chiefs.

Helena Strauss: Once human, Helena is now a vampire and married to Niccolo DiConti. She has a half-vampire daughter, Matty, who is destined to marry Andrus's son, according to Cimil.

Matty: The infant daughter of Helena and Niccolo, destined to marry Andrus's son.

Niccolo DiConti: General of the Vampire Army. Now that the vampire queen is dead, the army remains loyal to him. He shares power with his wife, Helena Strauss, and has a half-vampire daughter, Matty.

Reyna: The dead vampire queen.

Roberto (Narmer): Originally an Egyptian pharaoh, Narmer was one of the six Ancient Ones—the very first vampires. He eventually changed his name to Roberto and moved to Spain—something to do with one of Cimil's little schemes. He now spends his days lovingly undoing Cimil's treachery, being a stay-at-home dad, and taking her unicorn Minky for a ride.

Tommaso: Once an Uchben, Tommaso's mind was poisoned with black jade. He tried to kill Emma, Votan's mate, but redeemed himself by turning into a spy for the gods.

Tula: The incorruptible administrative assistant at Immortal Matchmakers, Inc.

About the Author

 Mimi Jean Pamfiloff is a *New York Times* & *USA Today* best-selling author of Paranormal and Contemporary Romance. Her books have been #1 genre sellers around the world. Both traditionally and independently published, Mimi has sold over 500,000 books since publishing her first title in 2012, and she plans to spontaneously combust once she hits the one million mark. Although she obtained her international MBA and worked for over 15 years in the corporate world, she believes that it's never too late to come out of the romance closet and follow your dream.

When not screaming at her computer or hosting her very inappropriate radio show (*Man Candy Show* on Radioslot.com), Mimi spends time with her two pirates in training, her loco-for-the-chili-pepper Mexican hubby, and her rat terrier, DJ Princess Snowflake, in the San Francisco Bay Area.

She continues to hope that her books will inspire a leather pants comeback (for men) and that she might make you laugh when you need it most.

Sign up for Mimi's mailing list
for giveaways and new release news!

LEARN MORE:

mailto: mimi@mimijean.net

www.mimijean.net

twitter.com/MimiJeanRomance

http://radioslot.com/show/mancandyshow/

www.facebook.com/MimiJeanPamfiloff

ANSWERS TO THE QUIZ:

1. Dear gods, I am so very grateful that Mimi has decided to write a spin-off of the Accidentally Yours Series because:

> A. It gives me an excuse to continue sending Mimi unicorn-themed items (such as hand-crocheted hats, earrings, headbands with uni-horns, stickers, socks, "I don't believe in humans" T-shirts, "I fucking love unicorns" pint glasses, and underwear) as well as all of the unicorn-related posts I find on Facebook.

> B. It did not sit well with me that Andrus, Tommaso, Belch (the God of Wine), Bees, the Goddess of Forgetfulness, Gabran, K'ak, Zac, Sentin, and all of the other immortals I've grown to love have not found their mates. Where's the justice in that?!

> C. I do not buy for one moment that Cimil can be reformed, but I'm excited to watch her try.

> D. Men in leather pants with turquoise eyes make me wetter than a tadpole.

> **ANSWER: ALL OF THE ABOVE**

2. I predict that during the IMMORTAL MATCHMAKERS, INC., series, we will discover the following about Minky the unicorn:

A. She's not real and never has been.

B. She dreams of becoming a porn star.

C. She is secretly in love with one of the gods.

D. Minky isn't a unicorn, but another species enslaved by Cimil for her own personal amusement.

ANSWER: ALL OF THE ABOVE

3. Cimil hates clowns because:

A. They are evil.

B. They are evil.

C. They are evil.

ANSWER: Need you really ask?

Made in the USA
Monee, IL
24 June 2020